---- ★ ----

I COULD UNDERSTAND CLEANING UP THE HOUSE

I could even sort of understand making up the bed and tucking Jane in it. But I could not understand why he would take the clothes Jane was wearing.

Unless there was blood on them.

The killer's blood?

I had the feeling—a most unpleasant feeling, which I have had in a few previous cases, a most unpleasant feeling, which usually proves true—that this killer was smart.

That this killer wasn't going to be caught fast.

That this killer may not be caught at all.

---- ★ ----

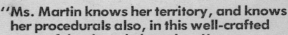

"Ms. Martin knows her territory, and knows her procedurals also, in this well-crafted story of death and obsession."
—*Dallas Morning Post*

THE MENSA MURDERS

LEE MARTIN

W❂RLDWIDE®

TORONTO • NEW YORK • LONDON
AMSTERDAM • PARIS • SYDNEY • HAMBURG
STOCKHOLM • ATHENS • TOKYO • MILAN
MADRID • WARSAW • BUDAPEST • AUCKLAND

THE MENSA MURDERS

A Worldwide Mystery/March 1993

First published by St. Martin's Press, Incorporated.

ISBN 0-373-26115-2

This book is dedicated to my oldest daughter,
Virginia Lee Webb, who, since the age of fifteen,
has served as my first critic and first editor.
If she says there is something wrong with a
manuscript, I don't waste time arguing.
I just go find out what's wrong and fix it.

ONE

DR. HABIB WAS SHOUTING at me.

This was not a glorious start to a fine Wednesday morning in late October.

I held the phone about a foot from my head. I could still hear him, quite clearly. So could Dutch Van Flagg, across the width of his desk and my desk from me. So, I suspected, could Nathan Drucker, whose desk was in a far corner.

Dr. Habib was shouting about Jane Stevenson.

What did *I* do? It wasn't a case at all. Can't a quiet middle-aged lady—a *sick* quiet middle-aged lady—die quietly in her own bed without the deputy medical examiner getting hysterical about it?

All *I* had done was try to calm a rather hysterical friend. A casual friend at that, somebody I'd known just a few weeks.

It was yesterday, about two o'clock in the afternoon, when Beverly Hart called me. Bev is Dr. Habib's new secretary. His own secretary, so why wasn't he shouting at her instead of shouting at me?

Bev called and said, "Can you meet me somewhere for coffee?"

I don't drink coffee anymore. But if Bev just wanted coffee she could drink it at her desk. "What's wrong, Bev?" I asked, and she promptly burst into tears.

When people cry at my desk I can hand them a Kleenex. When people cry at me over the telephone I feel very awkward because I don't know what to do. So I said, "Where do you want me to meet you? Your office?"

"Not my office," she said quickly. "Oh, I don't know." She snuffled, blew her nose, went on crying.

"That yogurt place on Camp Bowie?" She ought to know the place by now, I thought. It's right around the corner, just a block or two from T-Com—the Texas College of Osteopathic Medicine—where Bev had been working in the medical examiner's office for just over seven weeks.

A muffled rustling sort of noise. Then she chuckled through her tears. "I was nodding. I forgot you can't see me. Yeah, that's okay. I know the place you mean."

"Twenty minutes?"

"Yeah. Yeah, sure."

It ought not to take me twenty minutes to drive there, I thought; it's barely three miles—well, maybe four or five—from my office. But there's that awful intersection where Camp Bowie and University get in each other's way, and traffic blocks up. Times I've had to sit for ten to fifteen minutes, right there at that one intersection, moving about two car lengths with every light change, and I've read the bank sign at the corner so many times I see it in my sleep. Fortunately they change it every now and then.

Bev was there before I was, in a neat navy blue suit and frilly white blouse that made her look vaguely like Lois Lane. She'd actually bought coffee, black, which she was stirring drearily, over and over, with a little pink-and-white plastic stick.

Her eyes were red-rimmed. It appeared that when she'd tried to wash off the evidence of tears her makeup went with it, so that she was quite pale and every separate freckle seemed to stand up from its background. "Sorry I'm such a drip," she choked, and at once began to cry again, one hand clenched in her dark auburn hair and the other half covering her face.

This I had expected. I got the box of Kleenex out of my purse—that's one of the reasons I have such a large purse—and set it on the little round table in front of her. Then I went and bought a small dish of chocolate frozen yogurt, in case the management didn't approve of people occupying tables and not buying anything, and went and sat down to wait for Bev to get through crying.

She went on crying. The teenager who served the yogurt kept staring in our direction and then looking away.

Finally Bev stopped, snuffled a couple of times, and said, "It's Jane?"

There had been a questioning note in her voice, as if I ought to know who Jane was. I did not. I waited.

"My sister, Jane. Jane Stevenson. She died this morning."

I made conventional noises, which Bev hardly heard. She went on talking. "Actually she didn't. Die this morning, I mean. She died sometime over the weekend. Probably Saturday night. But nobody knew... I *could* have gone over there Sunday. I even thought about going. I usually do go there on Sunday—not every Sunday, I mean, but when I go, I go on Sunday. So why didn't I?"

She managed not to cry again. "I really meant to go over there Sunday, but... Oh, let's face it, she was *tiresome,* the kind of person you get tired of if you listen to her very long. She always has been. I took her on vacation last year and got back tireder than when I left, just from coping with her. She was always complaining, she always felt so bad... but... but she really *did* feel bad. She was sick. She had congestive heart failure. Do you know what that is?"

I didn't, exactly.

"Well, I don't exactly know either. She'd had heart trouble all her life, just about, but it was getting worse. She was always swollen. Her wrists and ankles and face were swollen all the time, and she could get out of breath walking from the bedroom to the kitchen. There wasn't anything anybody could do about it, short of a heart transplant, and you don't run to heart transplants on a clerk's salary. Lately she'd started insisting she was going to get well, but I could tell she didn't believe it. She'd say that for a minute and then complain for five. So I could tell she didn't believe what she was saying.''

"She was a clerk?"

Bev blew her nose and nodded vigorously. "Yeah. In the water department. She loved working there. You know where their office is?''

I knew. It was on the lowest level of that gorgeously space-inefficient city government building; the water department clerks could look from their desks out onto a central pool, which sometimes had a fountain and sometimes didn't, depending on whether anybody had turned it on or not.

"She said she could breathe there. About the only place she could breathe, anymore. When they turned the fountain on . . . all those negative ions, she used to say. But of course it was just a matter of time until . . ."

"So it didn't come as a surprise," I said.

Bev shook her head. "No. Except . . ."

"That's really the worst kind of death for everybody," I said. "People talk about sudden death being bad—and of course a sudden death is always unexpected—but when it takes so long, everybody just wishes it would be over with, and then when it is people feel guilty..."

Bev chuckled, snuffled, and blew her nose again. "I don't feel guilty. That's not it. It's just..." She shook her head. "Deb, you're not going to believe this."

"Try me."

"I don't...I don't think she died naturally. I don't think she died of heart failure. I think she was murdered." She wiped her eyes. "I knew you wouldn't believe me."

"I didn't say—"

"I know you didn't. But it's true, isn't it? You don't believe me."

"Stop telling me what I think," I said without rancor. "I don't know what I think. You haven't told me anything at all about it. I can't form an opinion on no evidence."

"I thought you would probably know about it. The police were out there."

"Bev," I said, "there are about nine hundred sworn officers on the Fort Worth Police Department. If I tried to read everybody's reports I'd never have time to do anything else. All I know about it is what you're telling me. I don't know if you're right or wrong, because I don't have anything to go on. If you can tell me—"

"Yeah." She fiddled with the strap of her purse, drank a sip of coffee from the white foam cup, and made a face. "I forgot to put sugar in this. Well. Where to start? It was yesterday morning."

"I thought you said Saturday."

"Saturday was when she died. Yesterday morning was when they found her."

"Okay," I said when she paused. I waited. Bev didn't say anything. She sipped absently at the coffee, apparently oblivious now to its lack of sugar. Finally I started to ask, "So who—"

"Her boss found her," Bev said, jumping as if she had forgotten a conversation was in progress. "Doris Cupp. She works at the water department. Well, Jane has been sick a lot, but she's always been real good about calling when she's not going to make it in. So when she hadn't come in by nine-thirty, Mrs. Cupp started trying to call her. She didn't answer the phone, and Mrs. Cupp got worried about her and went over to the house. She knocked on the door, and then she went around and knocked on the windows, you know like you do when you're trying to wake somebody up? She said she could see Jane through a window."

"Where was she? Jane, I mean."

"In bed. Covered up. Lying on her back with the sheet and blanket up to her neck."

"You mean Mrs. Cupp could look through a window and see her in *bed?*" It seemed to me even the most careless woman, living alone, would be sure she wasn't quite that visible. Not unless she lived so far out in the country she could be certain of no prowlers.

Bev nodded. "In bed. Mrs. Cupp was outside her window by the rosebush."

"Wasn't Jane scared to be seen—"

"Of course she was," Bev interrupted. "Normally it would have been impossible to see through the window at night. She hated living alone. She just hated living with Zack worse than she hated living alone, him and his awful cigars. And I couldn't ask her to come live with me, not with Larry and the kids—"

"Okay, so Jane was in bed and Mrs. Cupp could see her there. That must mean the curtains—"

"She has—had—those frilly dotted swiss things," Bev interrupted again. "You know, they're real sheer. And window shades, not blinds or anything. Usually at night she lowered the shades, but..." She drank some more of the coffee. "Well, anyway, Mrs. Cupp could see her. So she banged on the window and of course Jane didn't stir, so Mrs. Cupp thought she might have had a heart attack or something—that was kind of to be expected, you know—and so Mrs. Cupp went around and checked the front door and it was locked and then she went around to the back door and tried it and it wasn't locked, so she went in to see if she could wake Jane up and...and she said as soon as she saw her she knew she was dead, but she, you know, touched her and she was...she was cold and stiff.''

''And this was about what time?''

''Almost exactly ten o'clock. Ten in the morning, I mean.'' On this, she sounded quite certain.

''What size woman was your sister?'' I asked, thinking that rigor mortis takes anything from eight to twenty-odd hours to set in all the way, so what time did she die?

''My height, about,'' Bev said.

I'd guess that to be about five-six.

''She was heavier, though. Maybe, I don't know, she was a big woman. Two hundred forty pounds? That sounds like too much. But she wore about a size twenty-four.''

That kind of overweight is not strongly recommended for a woman suffering from congestive heart failure. Actually, it's not strongly recommended for anybody. So far I hadn't heard anything that would make me suspect anything other than natural death.

''So she—Mrs. Cupp, I mean—called the police, then she called me. From a neighbor's house, because she locked the back door coming in, and then when she went back out the front for some air—the house, you know, smelled kind of bad—the front door closed behind her and automatically locked. I...I managed to catch Sanchez just going out there, and I asked him to take me. He didn't want to, but I told him it was my sister and he said okay. You know Sanchez, don't you?"

I nodded. If there had been a murder, Gil Sanchez, an investigator for the medical examiner's office, should have spotted it. Or... "Did Habib go too?" I asked.

Bev shook her head. "Uh-uh. It was that new guy. Davisson. Do you know him?"

"I've heard of him." I hadn't met Davisson yet. He'd been in Fort Worth only three weeks. He was a qualified physician, but not yet a qualified pathologist, which meant he was sort of on probation as deputy medical examiner. If he passed his pathology boards he had the job, unless he pissed off too many people between now and then, and if he didn't pass his pathology boards he would be politely asked to hit the road, as others had been asked before him.

"Okay," I said, "so you and Sanchez and Davisson went over there, and Mrs. Cupp and the police were already there. Outside?"

"Uh-uh," she said. "The patrolman—I didn't get his name—had managed to get the front door open. He said the lock wasn't very good. He slipped it with his I.D. card."

Which meant Jane Stevenson didn't have deadbolts. Which in turn meant Jane Stevenson either wasn't very smart or was a lot more trusting than I am.

"So everybody went inside," I said. "And then what?"

Bev nodded.

I didn't consider that an answer, not to the question I had asked. "What did the house look like?"

"Just like it always does."

That also wasn't much of an answer. "What does it always look like?"

"Clean. Neat. Tidy. She's...Jane was always a good housekeeper."

"And she was in bed, in her nightgown, with the covers drawn up around her neck?"

Bev nodded again.

"And there was nothing at all out of the ordinary except she hadn't closed the shades or locked the back door."

"I didn't say that," Bev told me.

"Then what? What was out of the ordinary?"

"There was that, of course," Bev said vaguely.

"There was *what?*"

"I mean, she never even *used* the back door, and she *did* always close the shades, but if she was going to bed and she was having a heart attack or something, she might not think to close them, but I think she would have. Sanchez and Davisson said there wasn't anything wrong. She had a doctor's bill on the table and Sanchez called the doctor and he said it was completely expected, she could have gone any time."

"Bev," I said as patiently as I could, "I can see that it was a shock, your sister dying like that. But from what you're telling me I can't see anything at all unusual—"

"You didn't let me finish."

"Sorry," I said meekly, toying with my spoon and watching the yogurt melt. Because it was October, the air conditioning was off, but the front of the building was all glass, and it seemed nobody had explained October to the sun.

"Deb, she was laying on her back."

"Lots of people—"

"Not with congestive heart failure," Bev said positively. "She wouldn't ever lie on her back. She said she couldn't breathe lying on her back."

"But Bev, if she was . . . if she was dying, she could have just felt weak and headed for the bed to lie down and landed on her back and not had time to turn over."

"But she had time to pull the covers up."

I didn't say anything. I needed to think about this one.

"She'd have rolled over on her side before she pulled the covers up," Bev said. "I *know*. I told you I went on vacation with her last year. That's always what she did. In fact she wouldn't lie on her back at all. When she got in bed, she got in bed sort of sideways so she was lying on her side by the time she lay down. And one time, one night she was asleep and she did accidentally roll over on her back and she started gasping and woke up immediately."

"If she did that again and didn't wake up fast enough—"

"When she started gasping she also started thrashing around. The covers got all tangled up, Deb, she didn't lie down on her back and pull the covers up to her chin and die naturally. She just didn't. I saw that bed. She couldn't even get in it that neatly, much less die in it that neatly. Somebody put her there after she was dead. I'm certain of that."

"Did you talk to Habib about it?"

"Yes, but..."

"What did he say?"

"He said it was Davisson's case," Bev said bitterly. "Deb, she was my *sister*. I don't care whose case it is. I just want to know."

"Let me think a minute," I said.

Doctors, it is true, don't like to second-guess doctors. But there is such a thing as a second opinion, and although Bev's case was very weak, still she did have enough reason to legitimately ask for a second opinion. Maybe if we put it to Habib that way...

We talked a little more. In the end, I decided to accompany Bev back over to the medical examiner's office and tackle Habib myself. Not that Andrew Habib is the biggest cheese in the office; he's a deputy medical examiner himself, but it is Habib I usually work with, and he's at least got enough clout to get away with arguing with Davisson.

It's always safer to argue down than to argue up.

Habib, fiddling with a pencil held long-ways in his hand and for once not humming, listened intently. When I got through he said, "Who's going to authorize it?"

"You can—" I began.

"I can—" Bev began.

We both stopped at the expression on his face.

Habib shook his head. "Sorry," he said. "If there was any evidence whatsoever of suspicious death, or if she wasn't getting regular medical care, I could authorize it. But neither the police nor the examiners saw any reason to suspect anything wrong. She'd seen a physician—a heart specialist—four days before her death, and he said she was ready to go at any moment. So that doesn't give me any grounds whatever to order a postmortem. If it looked like murder I could, but it doesn't and I can't. And Beverly, you can't authorize a postmortem because you're not the next of kin."

"I most certainly am." Bev sounded outraged.

Habib shook his head. "Genetically, yes. But not legally. She was married."

"But they hadn't lived together since—"

"All the same, she was married. You find her husband—fast—and get him to request it, and I'll do it. Myself, if you want. But that's the only way."

Looking at Bev's tearful face, at my probably angry face, he added, "I'm sorry. But the laws have to protect a lot of people. And sometimes that's real inconvenient for other people."

"And sometimes people get away with murder because of it?"

"Sometimes they do," Habib admitted. "And always will. That's-just the way it is."

"Have you seen her body?" Bev demanded.

He shook his head.

"Well, why don't you go and look?"

"What good will that do? If Davisson didn't see anything, and Sanchez didn't see anything, and the police—"

"It wasn't a detective that went over there," I interrupted. "Just a patrolman. He took a couple of Polaroid pictures and that was all. I don't know who it was, but you know how inexperienced a lot of our patrolmen are. And Davisson—"

"Has seen bodies before," Habib said. "Besides that, I wouldn't exactly want to call Sanchez inexperienced."

I wouldn't either. But all the same, assisted by my knowledge that Habib is one of the most curious of mortals, I managed to talk him into going to look at the body.

I talked him into taking me along.

Bev decided she could do without this trip. I could well believe that. What I found hard to believe was that she could manage to work knowing her sister's body was in a refrigerated glass-and-steel vault three rooms away.

Normally the body wouldn't be in the morgue. Normally, after a death about which there is no question, the body is at once picked up by a funeral director—but here again the problem of locating Jane Stevenson's husband had gotten in the way.

The cold miasma of the morgue is more familiar to me than I wish it were. But this time there was nothing particularly horrifying to see. Just the flabby body, slack mouth, half-open eyes of an extremely obese woman with pasty complexion and gray hair in an unfashionable short cut. Nothing at all to indicate that she hadn't died peacefully in her sleep. No bruises, no cuts, no marks of any kind.

Habib shook his head. "There's no reason for this," he said.

"But Bev's a pretty good secretary, isn't she?" I said, in my most persuasive tones. "To keep her happy..."

Habib sighed. "Find the woman's husband. I'll see to it the state pays for it, but that's the best I can do.

You've got to find her husband and get him to re-quest it. Or at least okay it.''

"Somebody's got to find her husband anyway," I pointed out. "Somebody from your office ought to be—"

"Sanchez is on it," he interrupted.

"So I'll find Sanchez."

I found Sanchez and went with him, not checking in at my office so that they couldn't tell me to get my-self in and get on with my real work.

By about four-thirty Sanchez and I had located Zack Stevenson. It wasn't really hard to do; he wasn't a missing person, just a husband who'd walked out of a marriage neither he nor Jane particularly wanted anymore, who hadn't bothered with a divorce be-cause neither he nor Jane was interested in anybody else. He was driving a truck for Charles's Chips. His office gave us his route, and we just followed it. The enameled light brown truck was easy enough to spot.

Sanchez cravenly left the job of breaking the news to me. When I told Stevenson Jane was dead, he said, "Well, damn," with no particular show of surprise. He wiped at one corner of his left eye with his right forefinger and said again, "Well, damn. I knew that was coming. I tried to get her to let me move back in—wasn't no use her trying to look after that house alone, shape she was in—but she wouldn't think of it. Said what was over was over. I told her I'd sleep on the couch, I just wanted to help her, but she said she didn't need no—any—help from me. Said she was gonna get well and show everybody. I knew that wasn't going to happen and so did she.''

"Bev thinks somebody might have killed her," I said.

He stared at me, rather blankly. "Why would anybody do that?"

I considered it a legitimate question. It was one I had considered asking Bev. Cui bono? Nobody, it seemed, would be likely to profit much from this woman's death. A little bit of life insurance through the city—probably not much more than enough to bury her, because nobody was likely to want to insure anybody in her physical condition. She owned the house she was living in, Bev had said, but that might not be correct. Most likely Jane and her husband had bought it together.

I asked.

"It's in hers and my name," Zack said, "but what difference does that make? Jane was thinking about moving out, getting an apartment downtown where she wouldn't have any yard work to pay for, 'cause she sure couldn't do it herself, but she hadn't decided for sure. I told her if she decided to, I'd move back in till we could get the place sold, and then we'd split the money down the middle. Why do you want to know? I mean, what difference does that make? It's just a house. We finished paying for it last year. It wouldn't be worth much, not in that neighborhood. Anyway, nobody would have killed her for the house. They couldn't have got it if they did. It's my house, now she's dead. But it's not worth much. And we never did have no kids. Not with her heart like it was. The doctor said she dassent.''

"Was her heart always bad?'' I asked, wondering whether he would confirm what Bev told me.

Zack nodded. "Yeah. Had about fourteen things wrong with it. She had rheumatic fever when she was a kid, and that's when they found out there was other stuff wrong too. She always had to be real careful. Never could do much—when she tried to walk she like to turned blue.''

Sanchez asked about insurance. That was nice. It meant I didn't have to be the one to ask.

"What there is of it, I guess it's made out to Bev,'' Zack said. "Jane told me the way she had it set up her bills and funeral would get paid and then Bev would get what was left. That was okay with me. Bev was her kid sister.''

If Zack refused permission for the autopsy after I explained it, I would decide he was too good to be true. But he didn't. He just said, in a very worried tone, "Will her insurance cover it? 'Cause I can't afford—''

"It'll be taken care of," Sanchez told him, without going into detail.

"Then it don't make no difference to me," Zack said, "I just don't know what you 'spect to find. She's been dying all her life. Everybody knows her knows that."

He signed on all the dotted lines Sanchez told him to sign on, including one that turned responsibility for the funeral over to Beverly Hart. Sanchez and I went back in and turned the pieces of paper over to Habib.

"I'll get at it first thing in the morning," Habib said in a rather resigned tone, with a complete absence of humming, which I suppose meant he was not at all interested in this case.

I went and told Beverly. She thanked me and began crying again.

I still didn't ask her why anybody would want to kill her sister. I figured that first thing in the morning Habib was going to find out that nobody killed her sister, that Jane Stevenson had died a perfectly natural death.

That was what I thought.

And now, at approximately eight-ten on Wednesday morning, Dr. Habib was screaming at me over the telephone. Screaming at me that that was no expletive deleted natural death, that woman died of an expletive deleted broken neck.

TWO

THERE'S NOTHING like getting to a crime scene late, I thought crossly, and then I reminded myself it wasn't as bad as it could have been. This was by no means the first time in history a murder had gone down as natural death until somebody got to checking around.

There was Napoleon; from the moment he died, his death was rumored to be due to poison, but it wasn't until the last part of the twentieth century that anybody proved it, and even today who did it is up for grabs, although good cases have been made by various writers. Poison often works that way, though; it's so often undetected not because it is hard to prove, but because it is rarely suspected. A lot of murders-for-profit would never have been found out if murderers hadn't been so greedy they repeated the same method over and over again.

Then there was that woman in France, the babysitter they called the Death Angel. By the time somebody actually got suspicious enough to start to watch her, she'd strangled twenty-odd babies and small children, starting with her own. All six of them. Over a period of about fourteen years.

There weren't any crime scenes left when they finally caught on to her, except the newest one when they caught her in the act. Just a lot of tiny skeletons with crushed hyoids.

Crushed hyoids just like the one Jane Stevenson had.

Why in the world would anybody want to murder a lot of babies? It wasn't for profit; even the Death Angel's own children had no insurance. And it wasn't to escape the drudgery of child care; she would beg to be allowed to look after other people's babies. I couldn't imagine what her motive would be. But thank goodness, that wasn't my case.

Jane Stevenson was my case, and this looked about as motiveless as that.

Why in the world would anybody want to murder a dying woman? If—as seemed virtually certain—nobody was going to profit monetarily from her death? Assuming she wasn't a blackmailer, and water department clerks don't usually ferret out the kind of secret that could lead to blackmail.

A theft? A burglar who was caught in the act? But in this case why would she be found in bed . . .

This case—now it was a case—was making my head hurt.

I walked down to ident to see who could go back to the crime scene with me. Irene Loukas was, surprise, surprise, on leave. Not sick leave, not maternity leave, just a plain old vacation. She rarely does this; apparently she doesn't approve of vacations. For herself, that is. It wasn't a long vacation; the sign-out board said she'd be back tomorrow.

Bob Castle was leaning back in his chair with his feet on his desk, peering at latent fingerprints through that kind of magnifying glass that resembles a combination flashlight and minimicroscope. He says when you've got bifocals that's the only position in which fingerprints approach legibility. He didn't look as if he wished to be disturbed, and I didn't want to disturb him. The name on the fingerprint card he was comparing the latents to suggested he was about to clear a series of robberies.

So I asked Sarah Collins, who seemed relatively unbusy for an ident officer—she was filing fingerprint cards, which is nobody's favorite task—if she would go with me. Sarah had been in ident only about eight months, but she has several years of experience in uniform division. They tried her in intelligence, hoping to use her undercover, because she's got a lot of street smarts, but she turned out to be too memorable. She's the kind of woman who can attract wolf whistles when she's walking down the street in baggy blue coveralls, wearing a .357 magnum with a six-inch barrel and carrying a sawed-off shotgun. I think she's a mixture of black, white, Cherokee, and Oriental, which doesn't leave out much of anything that I can think of. She has curly red-brown hair, green eyes, and skin that looks like it's in a perpetual state of excellent tan, though she tells me she puts on factor fifteen sunscreen before she gets out of bed. She says I wouldn't believe how badly she sunburns. Actually I would believe it, but that's another story.

"You want me to ride with you, or just follow you out there?" Sarah asked me.

I shrugged. "Thing is, I don't know how much there'll be to do."

"I'd better follow you," Sarah said. "One of us might need to leave fast. Anyway, I'd rather arrive with too much gear than too little."

Having once been in ident myself, I knew what she meant by that. She certainly needed a camera: even though the body was long gone, we would want careful photographs of the rest of the scene. She certainly needed rulers and tape measures and graph paper, for crime scene measurements and sketches. She certainly needed evidence collection facilities, which meant two or three sizes of paper and plastic bags, boxes, labels, and so forth, as well as assorted tweezers, forceps, and plastic gloves. She certainly needed the equipment for developing and collecting latent fingerprints, which meant powders and sprays and tape and glossy cards and two sizes of cameras besides the one for the general photographs. She might need plaster of paris for footprints. She might need—

Oh, never mind. The point was she had all that stuff in the trunk and backseat of the ident car. And it was certainly easier for her and me both if she drove that car to the scene rather than taking the time to transfer all that stuff into, and back out of, the detective car I was driving.

Jane Stevenson's small frame house, white paint peeling from its clapboard siding, its rickety gray front porch dusty, was on a little side street off Rosedale, in what I considered a crummy part of town. That would strengthen the possibility that she had been killed by a burglar. Or maybe...

I crossed the small, unmowed, weed-grown yard, noticing the unpruned rambling roses that climbed the rickety trellis, in bloom again in October after summer's heat. Standing beside the porch swing, which hung forlornly by one chain, and fiddling with the key Bev had given me, I had a brainstorm I possibly would have had earlier if Andrew Habib hadn't been shouting at me.

Her telephone hadn't been disconnected yet. I waited while Sarah dusted it for prints—almost certainly an exercise in complete futility, in view of the fact that we knew the first officer on the scene had used it—then I called Habib.

No, Jane Stevenson hadn't been raped. How nice of me to ask. Didn't I have sense enough to know he'd tell me if she had been?

"Andrew," I murmured, "which one of us asked for an autopsy?"

I replaced the phone neatly on the cradle before he had time to yell at me. Not only had I one-upped him, but also I had used the term *autopsy,* which he hates, insisting it means surgery on oneself. He prefers the term *postmortem investigation.*

Notice he didn't ask, and I didn't expect him to ask, why I thought anyone would want to rape a singularly unkempt size twenty-four woman. I'd been to sex crime school, and he'd been a deputy medical examiner quite a long time. Rape victims—not necessarily in Fort Worth, but the ones you learn about in the sex crime schools—have ranged in age from two months old (yes, that is *months*) to ninety-four years and older, from sizes you'd think would be impossibly small (yes, the baby died) to sizes so big you'd think it would take a porno film star to reach the spot. Rape is not a crime of sexual passion. It is a crime of violence and hatred.

But it wasn't what happened to Jane Stevenson. So once again, I was left to try to think of a motive. You don't need a motive for conviction, of course, but figuring out *why* certainly helps to find out *who*.

I was standing in an old-fashioned, old lady's house. That bothered me, because I do not consider myself an old lady, not at forty-three, which was my age that day. My *exact* age. It was my birthday and nobody had even noticed, which hadn't exactly caused me to rejoice in the morning, even before Dr. Habib started yelling at me.

Anyway, I do not consider myself an old lady, and also I do not consider Bev, who is about two years my senior, to be an old lady. I knew that Jane had been just a year or two older than Bev. She hadn't been fifty years old. But her house suggested a woman of half again, if not twice, her real age.

I knew she hadn't had any children; her husband had told me that, and so had Dr. Habib, when he got through yelling about her broken neck. I knew she and Zack had lived here alone until Zack moved out—why, I did not know; all Bev had told me, when Dr. Habib let me talk to her again after he got through yelling, was that it was by mutual agreement, and I hadn't asked Zack. I did vaguely remember Bev saying something about Zack's cigar smoke as a factor.

This house looked as if she had inherited it, furnished, from her grandmother. Zack had told me that they had bought it together.

But it still looked like an old lady's house. Maybe they bought it furnished? Maybe they bought it and then she filled it with inherited furniture? A front room, all dark old furniture and doilies on every flat surface. Lamps that looked as if they had never been turned on, with frilly paper shades that still had their original cellophane.

It was a living room-dining room combination. The living room area was to my left as I stood in the front door facing inside. The dining area, to my right, had four uncomfortable-looking polished wood chairs around a would-be dainty wood table, polished to a high gloss. The only things on the table, besides a stack of library books, were a white doily and the black dial-type telephone from which, as I had expected, Sarah had lifted no usable latents. At the windows, frilly white dotted swiss draperies, slightly too long, hung so that they dragged the floor below the tiebacks.

The next room, confusingly, was the bedroom, which also served as a hall. That meant that to get from the kitchen to the dining area of the living room you had to walk through the bedroom, past the bed from which, presumably, Jane's body had been removed. Even that procedure had done little to disarrange the pink floral-print sheets with tight hospital corners or the blue blanket and white chenille bedspread tucked in at the foot. It all looked very binding, very uncomfortable, especially for a large woman. At the head of the bed, toward the wall separating the bedroom and the kitchen, there was no bedside stand of any kind. Apparently she'd used the windowsill for that. Nothing was on it now except a small wooden coaster with a cork insert. Had she usually kept a glass of water there? Was the glass under the bed?

I looked. It wasn't. That might or might not mean anything.

Against the opposite wall, so that the traffic pattern from the front room to the kitchen led between it and the bed, was a massive dark oak bureau, the long, low kind with a mirror bolted to it. A hairbrush, a comb, and a steam vaporizer were on top of the bureau—more precisely, on top of a violet-embroidered dresser scarf that ran the length of the bureau.

Last time I saw an embroidered dresser scarf while I was on a case, its owner was eighty-nine years old.

To the right of the bureau was the open door to a closet. Not a walk-in closet, just a small closet crowded with hanging clothes and shoes.

The sourish odor of illness and the old rose fragrance of sachet mingled with the indescribable and unforgettable scent of death. Loose sphincters had released body fluids; decay had unmistakably begun. Not exactly to escape the smell, I stepped into the kitchen.

Brown linoleum peeling off the tar paper that covered the subflooring. A clean black-and-white tile counter, several small squares of tile missing, the empty spaces filled in with some sort of mortar or plaster. A clean sink, white porcelain, with all the gloss diligently scrubbed off. An old, but clean, pale green gas range. An old, but clean, white refrigerator, also gas. I couldn't remember the last time I'd seen one of

those. A yellow Formica table, restaurant-style salt
and pepper shakers on it, two metal and yellow plastic chairs pulled up to it. Apparently this was where
she ate, instead of the formal dining area. That made
sense. I'd do the same thing, if I had a house laid out
this way. Except of course, that I wouldn't have a
house laid out this way. There was nothing on the table or counter that didn't obviously belong there,
nothing at all in the sink, nothing on the stove but an
empty, clean drip coffee pot. A clean, tidy kitchen,
bearing the same message the front room did: a very
old lady lived here.

The bathroom opened off the kitchen, to the left as
I faced the backyard. Faded pink towels hung neatly
on towel bars. A half-used bar of soap was in a soap
dish by the sink. I opened the medicine cabinet; it
contained a not-unexpected array of prescription
medications with names I didn't recognize, as well as
a few I did, and some of the most common over-the-
counter remedies—aspirin, ibuprofen, deconges-
tants, Vicks Vaporub. Jammed in the space between
the bathtub and the sink was a closed pink wicker
laundry hamper.

The bathroom floor was covered with chipped
brown linoleum, just like the kitchen. A faded pink
bathmat, slightly rumpled, was the first sign of dis-
order I had seen in the house.

I bent over to look at it more carefully.

It covered a spot of nearly black dried blood. Or rather, something that looked like a spot of nearly black dried blood.

It might mean something. It might not mean anything at all. Jane Stevenson wasn't fifty when she died. She might have been menstruating. She might have gotten up during the night to go to the bathroom and not noticed that she was dripping just a little.

But as clean as the house was, a thing like that had to have happened just before she died; otherwise she'd have seen it and cleaned it up.

Wondering where Sarah was and what she was doing, I returned to the kitchen and opened a drawer to look for a table knife. A camera strobe flash from the front of the house let me know where Sarah was and what she was doing. There was no use bothering her about this quite yet.

Using the knife to avoid complicating the scene by leaving my own fingerprints, I hooked open the door of the small linen closet above one end of the tub. That was the only closed thing in the bathroom except the hamper and the medicine cabinet above the sink.

There were no sanitary pads or tampons in there.

Jane Stevenson was nearly fifty and very unhealthy. She could have been menopausal, or she could have had a hysterectomy. Or she might be, for that matter, a perfectly functional female who might have been caught unawares, having used up one box and not yet purchased another. I am told that when you're approaching menopause your period likes to play gotcha. I expect to be learning all about that for myself in a few years; for now, I'm quite content to take other people's word for it.

One spot of blood. Only one. Jane's, or somebody else's?

Sarah would have to collect it, fill out the lab sheet, and send the single spot of blood to the lab, which would eventually tell us whether it was human blood, what type it was, and whether it contained the differentiated epithelial cells that would tell us for sure it was menstrual blood. Or whether it could be from a nosebleed or a scratch somebody might have gotten in a struggle with a sick, frightened woman fighting for her life.

I headed back toward the front of the house. Sarah's strobe flashed again, and I saw a glint, an answering flash, from the hem of the draperies. The reflection was instantly gone, but I remembered where I had seen it. I walked toward the spot and kneeled to investigate, pushing the frothy hem of the draperies aside.

A pair of glasses. Gold-rimmed bifocals, the right lens cracked, the wire of the right earpiece bent.

I called Dr. Habib again, hoping he wouldn't hang up on me for my earlier rudeness. "Three questions," I said as soon as he answered. "Was she on her period, did she do any bleeding otherwise, and did she have a bruise or abrasion of any sort near or behind her right ear?''

''She wasn't on her period,'' he said quickly, ''and she had no injuries that would cause bleeding—and I specifically include the nose. She wasn't bleeding. The other…hmm. I didn't…I don't think I noticed. Hmm. Let me check on that. Sounds like you're onto something. You got a number where I can reach you?''

He was *hmming*. He'd gotten interested. That might help. I gave him the number penciled onto the middle of the dial. ''I'll call you back,'' he said.

He did, about one minute and forty-five seconds later. ''Not much of one,'' he said. ''Not enough to cause death. I told you she didn't do any bleeding, and I already gave you—''

''The cause of death,'' I agreed. ''I know that. Not much of a what?''

''What did you ask about?'' he inquired, with an exaggerated imitation of patience.

''Bruises *or* abrasions, O great guru,'' I said. ''So which?''

''Both,'' he said sweetly. ''Slight bruise, slight abrasion. Behind her right ear, also on the right side of the bridge of her nose, up beside her eye. Looks like maybe somebody tore or knocked her glasses off.''

''Would you swear to that in court?''

''Swear to a maybe?''

"Swear to a maybe."

"Yeah, I guess. If you want me to. But why?"

"Because I'm holding the glasses in my hand," I said, and hung up. Actually, the glasses were still on the floor three-quarters of the way under the hem of the draperies, waiting for Sarah to photograph and maybe fingerprint them. But I wasn't exactly lying. *Figuratively* I was holding them in my hand.

So Jane wasn't on her period, which meant that whether she was menopausal was no longer of any interest to me. She hadn't been bleeding at all.

Unless I was wrong about what that spot was—and I've seen enough blood old and new that I was pretty sure I could recognize it—*somebody* had done some bleeding within the last three or four days.

I didn't blame Sanchez or the patrol officer on the scene (whoever that had been) for missing the glasses, for missing the single spot of blood. I might well have missed the glasses myself, if I hadn't been standing in just the right position when Sarah took just the right picture. I'd like to think I'd have found them, but I don't really believe I would have.

There was just no reason to look for them, no reason to look for that single spot of blood. Not when there was no other sign whatever of any violence or struggle. Not when a woman known to be slowly dying was in bed, lying on her back, in her nightgown, with the covers up to her neck.

In her nightgown. Not in her robe. Where *was* her robe? Did she even have one?

It didn't make sense that she would let anyone into the house when she was wearing nothing but her nightgown. Even another woman. Would I let Susan Braun, who is my closest friend and besides that is a physician herself . . . well, I don't think I would. Not that it would bother me. I mean, when I was in bed with the baby and Susan came in, I didn't feel compelled to get up and put something on, but if I was going to the front door to open it, even if I was 100 percent certain it was Susan there, I would put on a robe.

I think.

Zack?

I'd already ruled out Zack. Maybe I would need to unrule him out. But his surprise had seemed genuine, if understated, and I didn't think he was that good an actor.

What if . . . What if. What if. What if.

What if the person who had almost certainly put her in the bed and pulled the covers over her had also put the nightgown on her? I couldn't think of any logical reason for anybody to do that, even if they wanted us to think it was a natural death. I mean, given her medical history, she could die just as easily in her dress as in her nightgown. But on the other hand, whoever killed her might not know her medical history. In this business, it doesn't pay to take anything for granted.

I went to look in the laundry hamper. Maybe if I could find out what she'd been wearing earlier I could trace her movements during the day more easily.

In the laundry hamper I found a pair of white cotton panties, a white cotton bra, and a white cotton slip.

That was all.

That was *all*.

And that didn't make sense. Not unless I had missed something. I started back through the house, methodically opening every door to be sure I knew what was behind it. No. I hadn't been mistaken. She had no washer or dryer, no hidden staircase or door that might lead to a washer and dryer.

Maybe she washed by hand. I opened the back door to see if there was anything on the clothesline.

No. There was no clothesline for there to be anything on.

Look, no matter how tidy and clean she was, when she went out to do the laundry she didn't go in her nightgown. Even if she'd gone out Saturday afternoon to do her laundry and come home and put everything away, that still left the clothes she was wearing when she did it. So where were they?

Maybe she hung them back in her closet. Some people do that, if they decide the clothes can stand a second wearing. I don't, because they make the clean clothes smell kind of funny, but some people do.

I opened the closet door. With a mild mental shudder, I began to sniff at each dress, each blouse, each pair of slacks. It didn't take long. She didn't have many clothes. The closet was crowded because it was small, not because there was a lot in it.

By the time I got through, I was sure that whatever she had worn the last day of her life had not been hung back in the closet unwashed. A worn pink plush robe was there, too, and from its looks and smell I'd have been willing to bet money that it also had not been worn since its last washing.

Ergo, Jane had gone Saturday to do laundry—I'd have to find out where she had gone—and she certainly had been wearing something when she did it. Of course, there was the outside possibility that whatever it was, she'd washed it out by hand and dried it on a hanger and put it back in the closet. But somehow I doubted that too. If she'd hand washed a dress, or a shirt and slacks, then surely she'd have hand washed the underclothes as well, especially in view of the fact that far more people hand wash underclothes than streetwear.

The long bureau had two drawers, one above the other, both of them running the full length. They were wide and deep. The pulls were brass, so I didn't dare touch them until Sarah had dusted them for latents, because almost certainly whoever put the nightgown on Jane, whether it was Jane or her killer, was the last one to touch those drawer pulls.

I waited and dithered awhile and then asked Sarah to stop what she was doing long enough to come dust these drawer pulls so that I could open the drawers.

She did it, with much less grumbling than Irene would have done. "Nothing," she said.

"Unreadable?" I asked. That is usual on things like doorknobs and drawer pulls, because everybody touches them in the same place all the time and the prints stack up together like puzzles.

"Nothing, nothing," she clarified, and pointed with the tip of her fingerprint brush.

I still couldn't see anything. I am probably about due for bifocals myself, though I don't want to get gold-rimmed ones like Jane Stevenson had worn.

Sarah directed the beam of her flashlight on the top drawer pull. "*Now* do you see it?" she demanded.

Now I saw it. Watermarks, very small droplets, the kind you get if somebody washes something and then dries it thoroughly.

This drawer pull had been cleaned thoroughly since last time somebody touched it. I followed the flashlight beam to the second, to see the same thing. "That's all I'm getting," Sarah told me. "Somebody cleaned this place real good."

I WAS SITTING cross-legged on the couch, making lists, while Sarah worked around me, continuing to dust for fingerprints we both knew she wasn't going to find, continuing to take photographs that probably wouldn't tell anybody anything, continuing to collect evidence that probably wasn't evidence.

Somebody, for some reason that didn't make sense now and probably wouldn't ever make sense, had murdered Jane Stevenson. Whoever it was had then cleaned up all evidence of whatever struggle there'd been, except for that single spot of blood that he (I say *he*, though it could have been a woman; Jane was in no condition to fight back) had missed. My own guess was that he also had made (remade? Was it too bizarre to suggest that Jane might have had a boyfriend?) the bed, because in the first place I didn't think that Jane was physically up to making those neat hospital corners, and in the second place I didn't think Jane would have been comfortable sleeping in a bed that tightly made up. I wouldn't myself, and even though nobody but Susan still thinks I need to gain weight after several months of not eating about the time Cameron was born, I certainly don't wear anything approaching size twenty-four.

Having cleaned the house (missing the glasses, because they were Jane's glasses? Probably, but I'd have to ask Bev about that. And missing the single spot of blood. Why?) and made the bed and tucked Jane into the bed, so that with average luck nobody would ever suspect anything but natural death, he (she?) had then departed. Quietly? Or stood on the porch and had a loud one-sided conversation so that everyone would assume Jane was answering? Either one was possible. And either one would mean something different.

So. Things to do. Talk with the neighbors. Unless you've got a compelling reason to look elsewhere, that always had to be step one in a thing like this. Ask the neighbors what they saw, what they heard, being aware they might well have seen and heard nothing, and if they did see and hear anything they might not want to get involved.

Ask them if Jane ever had guests. What kind of guests. What they did. What kind of cars they drove. Hope you get some nosy old cat who saw everything and wants to tell it.

Ask when was the last time anybody saw Jane alive. And what she was wearing. And who she was with.

Try to find out where Jane did her laundry. If none of the neighbors know, drive to every laundromat in the area with a photograph of Jane and ask everybody there. And go back, or send somebody back, every day, because most laundromats are unattended, and the fact that the person doing the laundry on Wednesday never saw Jane doesn't meant that the person doing the laundry on Thursday or Friday or Saturday never saw Jane.

Try to find out what Jane was wearing Saturday, if anybody saw her, if anybody can remember.

Try to find out what Jane was wearing on Friday, just in case she did her laundry on Friday and decided to lounge around in her nightgown all day Saturday.

Talk with Zack again. Have a very, very, very long talk with Mr. Zachary Stevenson.

I could understand cleaning up the house. I could even sort of understand making the bed and tucking Jane into it. But I could not understand why he would take the clothes Jane was wearing.

Unless there was blood on them?

The killer's blood?

And maybe—maybe—find out why Jane had told her husband and her sister she was going to get well. Even if she didn't believe it, and they agreed she obviously didn't, there must be some reason why she had said it.

A faith healer? Somebody who couldn't deliver and killed her so she wouldn't blow the whistle?

But if that was the case, why tuck her neatly into bed?

I had the feeling—a most unpleasant feeling, which I have had in a few previous cases, a most unpleasant feeling, which usually proves true—that this killer was smart.

That this killer wasn't going to be caught fast.

That this killer might not be caught at all.

Sarah was still efficiently if not happily processing the crime scene. She'd gotten to the stage of drawing pictures now. After checking to be sure there was still a guard at the front door, just in case the killer decided—unlikely but not impossible—to return, so that Sarah couldn't be taken unawares, I decided to go about my own work and leave Sarah to hers.

THREE

IT WAS A LITTLE after noon when I went to knock on doors. Noon—or for that matter any time during the day—is not a good time to go knock on doors in middle-class neighborhoods. In the rich neighborhoods the wives are often home, because the husbands make all the money and the wives try to busy themselves with clubs and organizations, which don't usually demand quite the same amount of time jobs do. In the poorest neighborhoods, both husband and wife are often home because nobody has either a job or the money to go anywhere to goof off. But in middle-class neighborhoods, most often nobody is home during the day—the husband and wife are both at work, the children are at school or at the day-care center. This, by the way, is why residential burglary, which used to be a nighttime crime, has moved to the daytime.

I couldn't decide whether this was still the middle-class neighborhood it had started out to be, or whether it had evolved—or devolved, perhaps I should say—into the class of poor neighborhood. What I was hoping was that there were enough old people around to be able to tell me something. Old people are usually at home during the day in any neighborhood, and like children, they tend to be observant. My guess was that Jane's house had been built sometime in the 1920s. She and Zack had bought it probably in the late fifties or early sixties. Late fifties, if they'd just finished paying off a thirty-year note; if it had been a twenty-year note, they could have bought it as late as the late sixties. That would make them, at a guess, the second or third generation in the house. If I could find some neighbors who were first or early second generation in their same-age houses, then I would find somebody who would be home all day.

Nobody was home on the left; the red tricycle on the front porch suggested people younger, not older, than Jane. Of course the tricycle could belong to grandchildren, but the motorcycle beside it probably didn't.

Nobody was home on the right. At least nobody came to the door. But there was a wheelchair ramp beside the stairs and a walker on the front porch. An adult-size walker, I mean, not one of those things for toddlers. I'd try that house again later.

That left the house across the alley on the back, facing the next street over, and the house across the street, along with the houses on either side of it. Would Jane be more likely to visit across the street or across the alley? That was a silly question to ask myself. I hadn't the slightest idea, and in view of her health and her work schedule I didn't have any reason to suppose she did much visiting either way.

Well, then, who would be more likely to notice her comings and goings? Most likely the people across the street; the people across the alley couldn't see anything but the back of her house and the back of her garage.

I went across the street and knocked on that door. A querulous voice inside—too tremulous for me to be certain whether it was male or female—said, "Go away. I never buy at the door."

"I'm not selling anything," I called. "I'm a police officer."

Silence, for a moment. Then a dragging noise. A woman who leaned heavily on a cane opened the door and peered out at me, lifting her other hand to push white fringe back from her eyes. "Police?" she quavered. "Is something wrong? Is it Roger?"

"No, ma'am," I said, wondering whether Roger was her husband, grandson, or dog. "I'm just trying to find out a little—"

"Janie died last week, you know," she interrupted. "Janie, across the street? You know?"

"Yes, ma'am, it's about Jane—"

"She was a lot younger'n me. I always thought I'd go first, but there, she got so fat, always eating sherbet she was. I told her, I said, 'Janie, if you don't stop eating sherbet and start eating real food, you'll die young.' That's what I always told her."

"Yes, ma'am—"

"She didn't ever eat annathing else, that I could see. Ever-time I went over to visit there she was, a-lying on the sofa eating orange sherbet in her good work clothes. She hung a towel draped over her blouse like a baby with a bib. Silliest thing I ever saw. Never a piece of meat did she have in that house after her husband left, never a green vegetable, always eating orange sherbet. You'd think she'd at least eat lime once in a while, but no. Always orange sherbet." She peered at me. "Do you eat orange sherbet?"

"Not very often." When *was* the last time I ate orange sherbet?

"What do you eat?"

"Oh, just about everything. But I need to ask you about—"

"There, and you're a healthy young woman, too. It just goes to show—"

"Ma'am," I said loudly, wishing I knew her name so I could call her by it, "I really need to ask you a few questions."

"Well, ask 'em then. What are you standing around talking about sherbet for?"

"Could I get your name?"

"What do you need that for?"

"I always like to know who I'm talking with."

"Well, you haven't told me who *I'm* talking with, now, have you?"

"No, I haven't. I'm sorry, I should have. My name is Deb Ralston." I dug my identification out of my purse and displayed it.

"Do you know Roger?" she asked me.

"No, ma'am, I don't."

"He's in the police department, why don't you know him?"

"There are nearly a thousand people in the police department," I pointed out. "I can't possibly know all of them."

"Well, you ought to know Roger. Roger Dennis. He's my grandson. You don't know him?"

"Oh, Roger Dennis," I said. "Yes, I do know him. I met him a few months ago." He'd helped me out on something and I couldn't, at the moment, even remember what. But I remembered the name tag that said Dennis, and I remembered the scrawled "Roger Dennis" at the bottom of a report.

"Then why'd you say you didn't know him?"

"You didn't tell me his last name."

"Well, I'm Rachel Dennis, what other name would my grandson have but Dennis?"

"I wasn't thinking, was I?" I replied humbly. The fact was, she hadn't told me her name or explained until now that Roger was her grandson, and even if she had, Roger could be her daughter's son. But I'd found out a long time ago that nobody ever gets anywhere arguing with old ladies. Sometimes I think I just can't wait to be an old lady myself, so nobody will argue with me. Then there are other times—like when my baby is howling at three o'clock in the morning and I have to get up at six to go to work, that I feel like a very old lady indeed, and I don't enjoy the feeling.

"Well, don't stand there all day," she scolded. "What did you want to ask me?"

"Could we go in and sit down? You don't look very comfortable."

Grumbling under her breath, she led me into a living room in which the furniture was as old as Jane's. But this room was alive; the china lamps were all turned on, and a clutter of knitting, magazines, Fort Worth *Star-Telegrams National Enquirers*, and *Weekly World News*es littered the coffee table, the couch, and the floor.

"Now what did you want to ask? Come on, come on, we haven't got all day!" She glanced at the clock. "'Guiding Light' starts in twenty minutes and I don't want to miss it."

"No, I'd hate for you to have to miss your television show," I agreed. "So I'll be as quick as I can. We're trying to find out a little more about what happened to Jane Stevenson—"

"I told you what happened to her! She didn't eat right and she died, that's what happened to her!"

"I'm afraid there was a little more to it than that," I began.

Rachel Dennis leaned over her stick, her face alight with anticipation. "What? You can tell me. I won't tell a soul!"

I believed that, and I believed pigs fly. But it would be in the paper that night anyway. "I'm afraid she was killed," I said.

"Killed! Killed how? That snoopy old lady boss of hers, she brought the police over, and that sister of hers showed up, but nobody said annathing about her being killed."

"We didn't know it to start with."

"Hmph! If Roger had a been there, he'd a spotted it to begin with."

"Then it's a shame he wasn't there," I said, "but of course he couldn't be everywhere. Now, Mrs. Dennis, can you remember the last time you saw Jane?"

"Going out the door on a stretcher, a'course."

"I mean before that. I mean the last time you saw her alive."

"Satiday. She was on her way back from doing laundry. Her washer broke down six years back, you know, and she never did replace it, 'cause she said she didn't have no place to put a dryer and she didn't like hanging it in the yard. Well, I can't blame her on that, these neighbors we got around here, some of 'em steal the clothes right off the line. Roger, he got me a dryer. He's a good boy, Roger is. Brung up right. Not like these kids nowadays with that purple hair."

"That's great," I said, hoping I sounded enthusiastic enough. "Do you remember what she was wearing when she got back from the Laundromat?"

Rachel Dennis abruptly ran out of words. She stared at me, a stricken expression on her face.

"If you don't know, that's all right," I said hastily. "Just if you do know..."

She shook her head. "She was carrying the basket. I remember seeing her head, so I know it was her, and I remember seeing the basket. That's all. I just don't think I did see what she was wearing."

"Do you remember anybody going to visit her Saturday afternoon or evening?"

She shook her head again. "Roger and Cheryl—that's his wife, Roger's wife I mean, Cheryl—Roger and Cheryl came and took me out for dinner."

"That must have been nice."

"Real nice. They took me to a Piccadilly's, and I had salmon croquettes with cream gravy. Cheryl, she's gonna have a baby. Be my first great-grandbaby. You think she'll take good care of it?"

"Sure she will. Roger wouldn't marry somebody who wouldn't take good care of a baby, now would he?"

"No. Guess he wouldn't, at that. Cheryl's a nice old-fashioned girl. I learned her to crochet. She learned real fast."

Cheryl's a smart girl, I thought, and asked, "Who all used to come visit her? Jane Stevenson, I mean. You seem to know pretty well—you noticed her boss and her sister, when they were there Monday, so you might know who else—"

Mrs. Dennis chuckled. "She useta have parties."

I don't mind admitting that startled me. I would not have expected Jane Stevenson to have parties. "What kind of parties?" I asked.

"Some club she belonged to. Mostly young people."

"Young people" to Rachel Dennis, I had already figured out, was likely to be anybody under sixty. "Women?"

"Men and women. Not loud parties. Usually, oh, call it fifteen or twenty people. Some of 'em would go out on the porch to smoke. Well, you know, with her heart, Janie couldn't let anybody smoke in her house. They were all nice and quiet. They'd start arriving around seven, seven-thirty, something like that, and usually they was gone by ten-thirty or eleven. Usually it was on Wednesday."

"You sure it wasn't a church group, then?" Wednesday night prayer meeting is not as common as it once was, but it's by no means a dead custom. Though to be sure, it's usually held at church.

"In Bermuda shorts and T-shirts with beer slogans on 'em? One feller used to run around in some kinda hat shape like a fox. Anyway, she didn't go to any church that I know anything about. I mean, she did go to church, but it was a kinda funny one. They useta sit around and call up spirits. She took me once and I said never again. I been a good Baptist all my life and I'm too old to change now.''

We talked a little while longer, but she didn't say anything more that was of any use. That was all right. She'd helped a lot already. Parties on Wednesday night, men and women in Bermuda shorts, the kind of cap that is most charitably described as ''cute,'' and T-shirts with beer slogans on them. A spiritualist church of some kind. Maybe that was why she expected—or claimed to expect—to get well? Definitely things I would have to check out. And probably somebody else would know where she did her laundry, what she had been wearing on Saturday.

Nobody was home on Rachel Dennis's right or her left. I'd try the houses on Jane Stevenson's right and left again later. For now I walked back inside the house, where Sarah was still working away. On impulse, I opened the refrigerator and looked inside.

Half a pound of cheese, plastic wrap over its original wrapper. Five cans of Miller Lite beer. A head of brown lettuce, two oversoft tomatoes, a moldy cauliflower. A bottle of Weight Watchers mayonnaise, a bottle of Seven Seas buttermilk dressing, a container of Weight Watchers margarine, a bottle of bargain-brand olives with a black-and-white label that said only PIMENTO-STUFFED SPANISH OLIVES IN BRINE, 16 OZ. In the freezer compartment, three half-gallon boxes sealed and one open and partially empty of orange sherbet.

Rachel Dennis hadn't been very far wrong, as far as Jane's eating habits were concerned.

"I'm through here," Sarah said, directly behind me.

I jumped a couple of feet. "What?"

"Sorry, didn't mean to startle you," Sarah said, sounding more amused than sorry. "I'm through here."

"You get anything that looks useful?"

Sarah grimaced. "Surely you jest."

The heck with it. I'd talk to the other neighbors later. Right now I was hungry. I'd put back on ten of the pounds my friendly neighborhood psychiatrist Susan Braun had been yelling at me about; now I had only twenty more to go to get back to my usual overweight condition, and I was working on them. My appetite, which had shut off about the time my highly unanticipated baby, Cameron, was born seven months ago, had finally cut back on, and it seemed I was hungry all the time.

Susan said that was fine, I was making up for lost time. Maybe. I was hoping now my appetite would shut off again when I got to the proper weight, because if it didn't I was going to look like a cow in about six months.

I helped Sarah load her equipment into the car and watched her take off. Then I locked the house, feeling thankful that we had a written consent-to-search from both Zack and Bev so that I didn't have to bother with search warrants, and I went hunting for the closest McDonald's, Burger King, or anything else of that ilk.

I called Bev from Sonic and asked her if she could meet me again at the yogurt shop. "I'm supposed to be working," she said.

"Tell the slave driver this is police business," I said, "and ask him if he'd rather I come ask questions at your desk. For crying out loud, Bev, you shouldn't be working right now anyway, and if Habib had an ounce of sense he'd know it."

"Oh, Deb," Beverly said, "you ought to know it's my idea, not his. What would I do at home? Sit around and cry? I might as well work. He won't mind if I leave. Five minutes?"

"Make it thirty," I said. I was on Belknap. Getting from there to the yogurt shop by T-Com could not be accomplished in five minutes.

Bev looked a lot more cheerful than she had on Tuesday. Apparently it was not the fact that her sister had been murdered that had her so upset as the fact that nobody believed her. Or rather, that nobody was doing anything about it. Now that we were doing something about it, Bev looked almost back to normal.

She knew about the spiritualist church. She was rather embarrassed about it, but she gave me the name of the pastor, who called herself Sister Eagle Feather, which gave me a pretty clear picture of the kind of church it was probably going to turn out to be. She told me Sister Eagle Feather lived over the church.

She knew where Jane did her laundry, because she'd driven Jane there a time or two when Jane felt too bad to drive.

She did not know about the parties, and seemed as surprised as I was. "If you were to ask me," she said, "I'd have been willing to swear she never went anywhere but work, church, the library, and the grocery store, and that she never had any visitors but me and a few neighbors."

This wasn't exactly getting us anywhere. I thanked her, consulted my list, and decided my next stop would be Sister Eagle Feather. And I was not going to call ahead. Not that I seriously suspected Sister Eagle Feather of killing Jane—con artists almost never turn to murder, though there are exceptions to just about every rule—but I had a hunch Sister Eagle Feather might be able to tell me something about the Wednesday night meetings at Jane Stevenson's house.

Also, I'd better have a talk with Zack.

And I needed to talk with Jane's co-workers and her supervisor, the one who had found her. What was her name again? Something like a tea party—Cupp, that was it, Doris Cupp. I figured my route on paper, which is always the easiest way to do it if I want to cover a maximum amount of territory in a minimum amount of time, and then set forth to see Sister Eagle Feather.

All right, I admit it. I was stereotyping. But let's face it, we stereotype because many stereotypes—those based on observation, not those based on prejudice—are very often accurate. In my sixteen-plus years as a police officer, I had met a lot of Gypsy and Indian fortune-tellers; very few of them were in fact either Gypsies or Native Americans, but it seems people going into the business of being fortune-tellers or fake psychics think people will be more impressed if they are Gypsies or Indians.

Sister Eagle Feather's church, a white frame building looking newly painted, did not have that kind of sign shaped like a hand that places like this so often have; in fact, it did not have a sign at all. There was a flight of stairs going up the outside left. I climbed them and knocked on the door.

A woman who was presumably Sister Eagle Feather opened the door into a combined living room and office. A desk, untidily littered with papers in stacks and piles, was to the right of the front door. A Commodore computer beside the desk was turned on, its monitor glowing with green letters that let me know a word processing program was in use.

Sister Eagle Feather—if this was Sister Eagle Feather—looked about thirty. And she looked quite a lot like my daughter Becky, who is, like the other two of my older children, adopted. Because Becky's approximately three-quarters Comanche, the first thing I asked was, "Are you Comanche?"

She nodded, looking both startled and pleased. "How'd you guess?"

I shrugged, not wanting to explain. "Just did. I'm Deb Ralston, Forth Worth Police Department. I need to ask you a few questions. That is, if you're Sister Eagle Feather?"

She no longer looked either startled or pleased. "This a shakedown?" she demanded.

"A shakedown?" I wasn't sure exactly what the word meant, though it connected in my mind with con games of some sort.

She looked at me in silence for a moment. "Never mind, it wouldn't be," she said abruptly, and turned away from the door. "Come on in. I don't have any coffee to offer you, but if you'd like some Red Zinger tea . . ."

"That sounds wonderful. I don't drink coffee anyway."

"Smart," she said over her shoulder, heading toward the kitchenette. "It's not good for you. Want some honey in it?"

"No, plain's fine."

"Hot or cold?"

"Whatever's easier. I like it both ways."

She came back into the front room, which was separated from the kitchenette only by some sort of pass-through, and set a mug down on a coffee table, which, like all the rest of the furniture, was heaped with books and papers. She retrieved a second mug from the desk, where it was perched precariously near the computer keyboard. Sitting down on the couch, she looked up at me. "Now. What do you want?" Before I had time to answer, she shook her head. "That sounds awful. Here, sit down." She shoved two or three stacks of books farther over on the couch to make room for me. "I'm not really that unfriendly. But that computer's giving me fits. I just got a new word processing program and I can't remember half the commands yet even *with* the keyboard overlay. And besides that, the police the last place I lived really hassled me. I had to leave before I went nuts or got myself into something I couldn't get out of."

"Why did they want to hassle you?"

She shook her head. "Some stupid bitch fortune-teller from the Northeast, Boston or someplace like that, came into town and took this girl, I think she was the police chief's daughter-in-law, for about fourteen thousand dollars. Well, I don't blame him for being mad at her, though he ought to have been mad at the girl, too, for being so stupid, but he lit out after everybody who was interested in any kind of alternative medicine or New Age stuff or anything. It wasn't fair and it wasn't right, but there wasn't anything to do about it. I didn't have the money or the energy to fight it.''

''Where was that?''

''Never mind the name of the town. It was in Louisiana a long time ago. And besides, the wench is dead.''

''What?''

She laughed. ''A quotation. That's one of my besetting sins. I'm always quoting things. That's from Shakespeare, or maybe it's Ben Jonson. I don't remember for sure, and don't ask me what play, because I couldn't remember if I had to. It just means what we're talking about happened a long time ago and a long way from here and it's not worth talking about now.''

''So why were you talking about it?''

''Cops,'' she said succinctly.

''Maybe if you didn't call yourself Sister Eagle Feather it would help. It's not your name, is it?''

"My name," she said precisely, "is Matilda Greenwood. And I really am a trance medium, but I don't suppose you believe in that."

"Not really," I admitted. "I don't even really know what it means. It's like channeling, isn't it?"

"Close enough. I suppose you don't believe in that either."

"No."

She shrugged again. "No reason why you should. Two-thirds of 'em are phonies. I'm not."

"Do you produce ectoplasm and stuff like that?"

"My, my, she does read. No. I do not produce ectoplasm or ghostly fingerprints or hands full of paraffin, and if you ever meet anybody who does—for real—I hope you'll call me, because I'd like to see it. But I really am a medium. And to be honest, I wish I weren't. It's tiring. I mean really tiring. I'd quit in a minute if I could."

"Why can't you?"

"You ever try to make a living writing books?"

"No."

"Well, don't, unless you want to live in a tent and eat acorns. Even when the income's almost enough, it's so irregular you spend your life playing catch-up— you know, where you pay June's bills in July, but you can't pay July or August until September is due. That kind of thing. People with irregular incomes live like that all the time. You don't want to try it."

"I wasn't planning on it. I play catch-up enough as it is. What kind of books do you write?"

"Health books. Trying to get people to stop filling their bodies with dangerous chemicals. And self-help books. Trying to get people to like themselves."

"Oh. Then why don't you work in a health food store or something like that?"

"On my feet eight hours for minimum wage? I've tried that too. I come home too tired to write. Was that what you wanted to ask me about?"

"We *have* gotten a little far afield. I was just curious. No. I wanted to ask you about Jane Stevenson."

She regarded me. "What about her? She wasn't in church Sunday, I can tell you that."

"She's dead."

"I'm not surprised. Her weight, with those heart problems she had—if I've told her once I've told her a hundred times, quit eating junk food and start walking. You know what she was eating? Breakfast, lunch, and dinner—orange sherbet. Once in a blue moon she'd eat a piece of cheese. Never any fruit, never any vegetables. I'll bet you three dollars she had scurvy. What did she die of?" Her feet now propped comfortably on top of a stack of magazines on the coffee table, she regarded me interestedly.

"Well, it wasn't scurvy," I said. "She was strangled."

Sister Eagle Feather—Matilda Greenwood—set her cup down rather loudly. "Are you kidding?"

"No, I'm not kidding. She was strangled, sometime over the weekend, probably Saturday night."

"And you want to know what she left me in her will and did I know about it and where was I Saturday night?"

"She didn't leave you anything in her will. You can tell me where you were Saturday night if you want to, but that wasn't why I came." I was getting a little annoyed at this woman's defensiveness. If she didn't want people to suspect her, why was she in this kind of business, using such a corny phony name?

"Saturday night," she said, "I was having a session."

"A séance?"

She feigned a shudder. "Please. A session. Here. There were three women with me. I can give you their names if you want them. Look, I'm not a phony. I'm a real medium. I give them the trappings—the name, the robes, all that garbage—because they expect it, and if they didn't get it from me they'd go to someone who would give it to them, and she might really be a phony out for what they would pay her."

"And they don't pay you?"

"Goodwill offerings. Enough to pay the rent and utilities. The writing does pay for groceries, usually. If I'm broke I tell them so and let them decide what they want to do about it, if anything. Look, my car is twelve years old and right now it's parked with two flat tires. My computer is a Commodore, a hundred and twenty-nine dollars new, and it's five years old. If I wanted to con somebody I'd do a lot better than this. What are you, some kind of fundamentalist Baptist or something?''

"I'm a Mormon," I said. "Well, actually, I'm not, because I haven't been baptized, but that's the church I go to when I go, and my son is a member."

She nodded. "A Mormon? No, you wouldn't believe in mediums. But I'll bet you three dollars Joseph Smith did."

"You may be right. I wouldn't have any idea. You like to bet three dollars on things?"

She shrugged. "A saying."

"Did you bet Jane Stevenson three dollars she could get well?"

"I did not. She was going to die. Very soon. I was working on getting her to stop being afraid of dying."

"You never told her she could get over it?"

"No. Telling her that would have been an evil thing to do. Why would I . . . Back up. Why are you asking this anyway?"

"I can't explain things in the middle of an investigation," I said rather stuffily. "Do you have sessions just on Saturday night?"

"Saturday night, Sunday morning..." She waved her hand languidly, sounding prepared to go on for a while.

I interrupted. "How about Wednesday night?"

"Sometimes. Why?"

"At Jane Stevenson's house?"

She sat up straighter, looked at me. "What in the world would I want to do that for? No. I've only been to Jane Stevenson's house once. It depressed me. I don't think I *could* go into trance there."

"You know anything about anybody holding any kind of meetings or parties there?"

"No. I can't imagine why anybody would want to. Really. I don't mean that as a putdown, but her house was really depressing. You know she was still living with all her grandmother's furniture? And she kept wanting me to call up her grandmother to talk with her."

"Did she ever?"

"Who? The grandmother? Once. Her grandmother told her she was a goop and she ought to have something better to do with her time. She—Jane, I mean—thought I made that up."

"Did you?"

"No. Well, not consciously. I don't think I did. *Goop* isn't a word I use, at least not that way. I use it to mean, you know, goop in the bottom of the sink. But I asked somebody what it meant used that way, and they told me there was this kids' book a long time ago about the Goops.''

"Well, I don't think it was that long ago," I said cautiously, vaguely remembering my grandmother calling me a goop when I cried over spilled milk.

"Whatever," Matilda—I really couldn't call her Sister Eagle Feather—said. "No. About your question, no, she never mentioned any kind of parties or meetings to me. And I certainly never told her she could get well. I told her exactly the opposite. But she'd been . . . secretive, the last few months. Maybe secretive isn't the right word. Sly, that's it, sly. I had the feeling she was up to something she knew I wouldn't approve of."

"Any idea what?"

"No. None."

"Do you happen to know what her divorce was over?" Maybe I was wrong, but I suspected if there had been more to it than Bev knew, this was the woman who would know.

"She wasn't divorced. Just separated."

"But did you know—"

"Because of his smoking, of course. I thought you knew that."

"His smoking?"

"Her husband smoked all the time," Matilda said patiently, "Cigars, at that. And Jane couldn't handle it. That wasn't just an excuse. She really couldn't stand to be around smokers. Somebody lit up once in my church, which I do *not* allow, and by the time I got over there to tell him to put it out or leave at once, Jane's face was absolutely purple. But her husband couldn't stop smoking. His wife was dying of it, but he just couldn't do without his tobacco."

"I've known people like that," I agreed. I'd want to find out if anybody else had been told a different reason. "Did she have any particularly close friends among, um, the members of your church?"

"No. Well, Winifed Hauksby, maybe, but I don't think they were very close."

"Don't you mean Winifred?"

"Winifed. Don't blame me, I didn't name her."

She found me Winifed Hauksby's phone number and address, and I thanked her and departed. I still don't believe in mediums, and I don't really think Joseph Smith believed in them either. But I was pretty sure that Matilda Greenwood believed in trance mediums. And she probably wasn't nearly as bad for the people in her church as a lot of other mediums would have been.

I'd try to talk to Winifed later; Matilda had been pretty sure she wouldn't know anything. I glanced at my watch. Zack should be parking his truck in just a few minutes. If I headed for the Charles's Chips warehouse now, maybe I could catch him.

But then I changed my mind.

With a baby at home, I'm a lot better about leaving on time than I used to be. And I'd just have time to get in, park my detective car, and dictate a few notes for a secretary to transcribe later, before it was time to go home. Zack Stevenson could keep. I didn't really think he was connected at all. I didn't really think it was a personal kill; my hunch was that we'd find out, maybe six months from now, that there'd been a burglar in the neighborhood who'd gone in, thinking she was asleep, and found she wasn't quite.

That sort of thing happens.

As I got off the elevator to head for my office, Millie—our new receptionist—looked at me with a half-kidding, half-malicious, expression. "You have a guest," she informed me.

"Thanks," I said, and strode on into the major case squad office, where I stopped short. "Oh, shit," I said aloud.

Ed Gough—that's pronounced *Goff*—turned to look at me sadly. "That isn't nice," he said.

"Ed, what are you doing here?"

You'd have to know Ed. He is a small man, about five-seven, with shaggy, graying hair. His clothes always look too big for him, and his expression always looks like his best friend died five minutes ago.

That's not why cops hate to see him coming.

Quite a few years ago, Ed, then in his early twenties, had raped and murdered his nineteen-year-old sister. She was wearing a green dress at the time. The courts, and the psychiatrists, agreed that Ed wasn't sane, either at the time of the deed or at the time of the trial, and Ed was packed off to a safe place, which kept him for quite a while. But seven years ago, neither to his liking nor to ours, they turned him loose.

For seven years Ed has worked at a particularly impoverished rest home, which I could only assume had hired him because they couldn't get anybody better for the money they could afford to pay. The idea of him working around helpless old people worried me. But as Dutch Van Flagg pointed out to me once, it should be perfectly safe. Bedridden old women don't wear green dresses.

For seven years Ed has showed up in the detective bureau to confess to every murder of a woman that has been reported in Tarrant County.

For the last few months, ever since I got back to work after the birth of Cameron, he has decided to pick on me.

He was still staring at me, his doggy eyes reproachful. "I'm sorry I said a bad word," I told him. "What are you here for?"

"I did it, you know."

"Did what?"

"Killed her. That lady. It was on the news today. I did it. I killed her. She had on a green dress."

"Ed," I said wearily, "she had on a nightgown."

"That was later. I killed her. She had on a green dress. You need to put me in jail so I won't kill anybody else."

"They won't let us put you in jail," I said. "I wish they would. I know you'd be happier there, and I'd be glad for you to be there. But they won't let us."

That wasn't even a joke. Ed had tried repeatedly, in the years since he had been released, to commit himself. The hospitals had always sent him back home with a handful of tranquilizers and instructions to behave himself.

"Can't you make them lock me up?" he pleaded. "I killed her. She had on a green dress."

"Ed, I have a friend who's a psychiatrist," I said. "I'll talk to her. Maybe she can figure out a way to get you locked up."

"Talk to her today."

"If I get a chance."

"Promise?"

"I promise. But Ed, you've got to go home now. I have to write reports."

"Go home?"

"Yes, you've got to go home."

"What if I see a lady in a green dress?"

"Look the other way," I advised, and got the tape recorder out of my desk to begin dictating my report.

Ed wandered off, looking vaguely dissatisfied. I hoped he was going to work.

How much trouble could he get into there?

FOUR

IN THE ELEVATOR, I meditated unhappily on Ed Gough. Someday, I thought, Ed Gough really is going to kill somebody else. And when it happens, the press'll be down on us like flies on you know what, demanding to know why we couldn't prevent it. And they'll be down on psychiatrists in the same fashion, wanting to know why *they* couldn't prevent it. And none of them will stop to think that it was their very own laws that made it impossible to keep Ed Gough locked up where he—and his potential victims—would be safe.

I wasn't exactly afraid of Ed Gough.

But then I am customarily armed.

And I rarely wear a green dress.

By the time I reached my car, I was feeling blue again. It was my birthday, and nobody, nobody, nobody at all, had noticed. Well, my mother had called and told me to come out on my next day off, whenever that might be, because she had something for me. And I didn't expect my fellow officers to care. But you'd think with a husband and four children—well, Cameron's not exactly old enough to think of these things—*somebody* would remember.

I sulked all the way home.

I was still sulking when I walked in the front door, but nobody noticed. My husband, Harry, sitting at his ham-radio table, went on talking to somebody in Nome or Fargo or wherever it was, and my son Hal wasn't indoors at all. Then, of course, I had to pick up my seven-month-old son Cameron and cuddle him, because he was cooing and holding his sweet little arms up to me. I couldn't possibly sulk at him, so I gave up on the sulking. It wasn't doing any good anyway.

I wasn't really being very fair. True, Harry seemed to have forgotten my birthday. But he had plenty on his mind without remembering birthdays—things like the job he had been out of since January, when he set a helicopter down on its side and landed in the hospital with a badly broken leg that hadn't healed right, as well as sundry other injuries, and things like the Social Security Administration, which had pointed out, reasonably I suppose, that although he might be disabled as far as flying a helicopter was concerned there were plenty of other things he could be doing, so they certainly couldn't certify him as disabled. The fact that he didn't know anything else didn't seem to matter.

So now he was frantically working on an M.B.A., which would qualify him for the administrative job Bell Helicopter had offered him, the one that he hadn't taken because he didn't figure he could do it. Also, since I was working during the day and he was in class only one night a week (which is more than it sounds like considering six weeks cover a normal semester of work), he was doing most of the housework except the cooking, which he is quite incapable of, and the laundry, which I had forbidden after he had poured an overdose of chlorine bleach into a load that didn't need any at all, and it ate all the seams out of my favorite slip. After that it just seemed easier to do the laundry myself than argue about it.

All right, he was putting the dishes in the dishwasher, vacuuming, and watching Cameron. But *he* thought he was doing most of the housework, and between that and the Napoleon Hill Institute of Management, which definitely believed in homework even if it didn't (as it explained in small print in its brochures) have anything to do with Napoleon Hill, he was having very little time for his beloved ham and CB radios and his small private airplane.

Apparently he'd gotten through housework and homework early today. Not only was he cheerfully talking on the radio but he had also shaved and had even changed out of his usual home-all-day garb, which consists of a torn T-shirt that was old when Nixon was Vice President—all right, President—and a pair of paint-stained khaki trousers. He was wearing clean khaki trousers, and he actually had a real-live buttons-down-the-front shirt over whatever T-shirt he happened to be wearing at the moment. Wow. He was dressed up.

Hal and his girlfriend, Lori, wandered in through the patio door, so intertwined I wasn't altogether sure how they were managing to walk. Hal had his usual out-in-the-stratosphere expression—sometimes I think he lives on Neptune—but Lori, who turned to slam the door on the dog's nose, was looking vaguely pleased with herself about something. They, too, were dressed up. That meant they had on clean jeans and clean matching T-shirts (this time the shirts were blazoned with pictures of the Goddess of Democracy at Tiananmen Square, which I thought was kind of nice), and they had laces in their sneakers. The laces were even *tied!* This was unreal. Maybe my birthday wasn't as forgotten as I thought it was.

It would help if somebody would say something to me, something beyond Harry's "Hi, Deb," Hal's "Hi, Mom," and Lori's "H'lo, Deb." Cameron, of course, merely gurgled, and the dog whined at the back door.

I opened the door, said, "Hi, Pat" while interposing my knee to barricade the door against the dog's usual insistence that he really lived indoors, and scratched Pat's ears. Pit bulldogs seem to have very itchy ears. Then I decided to go wash my face. I started to return Cameron to the playpen, but Lori reached for him and he smiled broadly at her, so of course I let her take him.

When I returned, May Rector had arrived. She lives down the street, and—at her request, not mine—she baby-sits Cameron whenever there is no member of the family available to do it. She smiled benignly, said, "Happy birthday, dear," and handed me a card.

I thanked her, probably sounding as puzzled as I felt—how did she know it was my birthday?—and Harry drawled, "We're going out to dinner, Deb. You wanta go do whatever it is you wanta do before we take off?"

I interpreted that as a suggestion for me to change clothes, comb my hair, and put on some makeup. But alas, even going out to dinner on my birthday I am required to carry my pistol. The crooks, you see, are never off duty, and they seem to know me well by sight. This, to some extent, limits what I can wear, unless I want to put the pistol in my purse, a location I consider a safety hazard.

The heck with it. I had no reason to expect to need a pistol tonight. I put it in my purse, which meant I could wear a reasonably feminine dress instead of a jacket designed to hide a shoulder holster.

Cattleman's. A private room, no less. Harry and me; Hal and Lori; my older daughter, Vicky, and her lawyer husband, Don; my younger daughter, Becky, and her medical-student husband, Olead. I started to worry about the cost of this shindig. Right now Harry and I were having to watch every penny. True, Olead Baker—who besides being a medical student is also a multimillionaire financial whiz kid—wouldn't even notice the price of the entire party, but Harry had been remarkably (or perhaps I should say unremarkably) unwilling to accept favors from his son-in-law.

That, I supposed, was the reason for the somewhat unnatural reserve with which Harry greeted Olead. Olead pretended not to notice. I was sure that was pretense, because Olead always notices everything. But Becky was chattering away about the baby she was expecting in November, and about the latest exploits of Olead's three-year-old half brother, whom Olead and Becky have adopted. Vicky was chattering about her son, Barry, born the same day Olead was acquitted of the charge of murdering his mother, stepfather, and three other people, and the uneasy moment apparently went unnoticed by anybody but me.

There were still a couple of chairs and place settings unoccupied. Evidently someone else was expected.

Someone was. My friend Susan Braun, one of Fort Worth's most outstanding psychiatrists, wandered in, with an extremely good-looking man I had never seen before ambling behind her. Susan, who was wearing an embroidered blue chambray shirt, a blue denim skirt with a lot of rickrack on it, and black cowboy boots, ran into a chair, stopped, backed up, blushed, and began to fiddle with her right braid, which as usual had worked loose from the bobby pins supposedly anchoring it on top of her head and was now dangling down beside her ear. "This is Brad," she announced almost inaudibly, reanchoring the braid haphazardly.

Brad—whoever Brad was—grinned amiably at me. "Hi," he said. "You must be Deb."

I nodded, knowing quite well I was staring at him. Harry stood up, assumed his best military man-of-the-world air, and extended his hand in that ritual men seem to have. "Harry Ralston," he announced. "Deb's husband. I'm a helicopter test pilot."

"Brad Graves," Brad replied. "Susan's fiancé. I'm a shrink."

That was the first time I had ever heard a shrink refer to himself, or herself, as a shrink, and I was a bit startled. But not nearly as startled as I was to hear him introduce himself as Susan's fiancé. Susan is, after all, forty-five years old; as she had never been married, I had no particular reason to expect that she ever would be.

That, I suppose, is stereotyping. Still, a forty-five-year-old woman—or man, for that matter—who has never been married is not overwhelmingly likely to change.

Anyway, you'd think she would have told me—unless it had just occurred. But you'd think she'd at least have told me she had a boyfriend.

Harry and Brad Graves had instantly plunged into a complicated discussion of something in the news, during which Harry called him "Dr. Graves." Dr. Graves waved his hand deprecatingly and said, "Brad, Brad. Aren't we all friends here?"

Actually we weren't all friends here. I wasn't at all sure I liked Brad Graves, though I'd have been hard put to it to explain why. He had a head full—slightly too full—of wavy silver hair, and he had blue eyes and a good, even tan and the slightly too sincere smile and slightly too firm handshake of a salesman or a politician.

All right, that wasn't just stereotyping. I was being prejudiced. Maybe that's what psychiatrists are supposed to look like. Maybe it's Susan who is unusual.

"What've you been doing lately, Deb?" Olead asked from the other side of me, and I turned my attention to him.

He wasn't just being polite. Olead is always intensely curious about my work. I started telling him about the new case and its attendant frustrations.

"I know a Jane Stevenson," Olead remarked. "But it's probably not the same woman."

"Probably not," I agreed, unable to think of a situation in which Olead, with his money and his school schedule, would have met this particular Jane Stevenson.

"Real...uh...fat," he said. "I think she works for the water department. Bad heart trouble. You can tell by looking at her."

"Same woman," I said, surprised.

"Hmm," he said thoughtfully. "I can't imagine why anybody would want to murder her. Well, actually, I can, but..."

"Olead, if you have an idea that might help me, give."

He shrugged. "It's not really a reason. She was sort of exasperating to be around. Whiny. That kind of thing. But nobody really kills people for being whiny."

"People will kill people for any reason or no reason, Olead, I've got to ask, where in the world did you meet Jane Stevenson?"

"At a Mensa meeting." He fiddled with his glass of water.

"A *Mensa* meeting?"

"Yeah," he said. "I know you know what Mensa is. I keep telling you, you ought to join it."

"I can't imagine what makes you think I would be eligible," I began.

"Ah, Deb," Olead parroted back to me, "I can't imagine what makes you think you *wouldn't* be eligible."

"Olead, I'm a cop," I said. "With a high school education at that."

"So what? That doesn't make any difference. Millions of millions of eligible people never join."

"How many?" asked Brad, who had stopped his discussion with Harry and was listening to Olead and me instead.

"Well, maybe not millions and millions. But millions, anyway. There a lot of people eligible who never join."

"It takes only people in the top five percent of intelligence," I said, "and I don't know what makes you think—"

"Top two percent," Olead interrupted, "and I know you. That's why I think you're eligible. I mean, look at it this way. If you take an across-the-board section of any hundred people in the world, two of them would be eligible. And don't worry about feeling nervous about taking the test. Everybody is. Even Isaac Asimov was."

"You want me to take a test *Isaac Asimov* was nervous about taking?"

"But Deb, he passed it."

"That certainly doesn't mean I would."

"Ah, Deb, take the test. I know you'd do great."

"Olead, I don't want to—" I stopped. "Jane Stevenson was in Mensa?"

"Yes. And if she could get in then I know good and well you—"

"Wait a minute, wait a minute, wait a minute, never mind about me," I said. "I want to talk about Jane Stevenson. She was in Mensa?"

"I already said she was."

"Let me think a minute. Her neighbor said she used to have something like parties or meetings at her house."

"That's right."

"Those were Mensa meetings?"

"Yes. On Wednesday, anyway. If she had meetings any other time then I don't know what—"

"It was Wednesday," I said, and fell silent.

"Is something wrong?" Then he laughed. "That was a stupid question, wasn't it? You're investigating a murder and I ask if something's wrong."

"I'm just thinking, two percent of all the people in Fort Worth, and the size of Jane Stevenson's house . . ."

"Well, nowhere near all the eligible people join. I told you that. But . . ." He looked at Brad and Susan. "One of you explain," he said. "You were there, too."

"You know what a SIG is?" Brad asked me.

"No, she doesn't know what a SIG is," Olead said. "Deb, a SIG is a special interest group. There are hundreds and hundreds of SIGs. People join Mensa and then they join SIGs. Okay, so the Fort Worth chapter of Mensa got really big, and it was just ridiculous to think of that many people all getting together very often, so we have...oh, it's officially a SIG, but really it's like a mini-Mensa chapter."

"Sort of a splinter group?" I asked.

"Sort of. It's composed largely but not entirely of people in the mental health care field."

"And Jane Stevenson was in it?"

"Yeah," Olead muttered, looking down at his plate, looking suddenly and unaccountably very unhappy.

"A water department clerk?" I demanded.

"Mensa requires intelligence of its members," Brad said. "What they call superintelligence. But it doesn't require anything else. Literally. Nothing else. It's got members in prison. It's got members who absolutely couldn't support themselves even if it was that or starve."

"But in that SIG? Mental health professionals?"

"There are many members of Mensa," Brad said, "who, in the vernacular, are more or less squirrelly. Remember, intelligence and sanity don't necessarily coincide. Jane wanted to be in our SIG. We couldn't very well throw her out."

"Well, I suppose we could have," Olead said, "but it would have been cruel and petty." He was still fidgeting, and Becky was gazing at him with a very worried expression.

"I think there's more to it than that," I said, looking at Susan, who seemed as unhappy as Olead.

"Well," Susan said, and didn't say anything else.

Waiters were serving our meal, and Brad said, "Why don't you come up to the office in the morning and let's talk about it then? That'll give me a little time to decide what I can say that will help you without, uh, overstepping the bounds of professionalism."

"So there is something more, something none of you are saying?"

"Yes," Brad said, and left it at that.

That was all anybody said about Jane Stevenson during dinner. Susan and Brad seemed as glad to be off the topic as Olead was, and I was really wondering what in the world an apparently inoffensive water department clerk could have said or done to provoke that much reaction from these people. These intelligent, well-educated, professional people.

But I tried to put it out of my mind. It was, after all, my birthday. And it would be absurd for me to have sulked all day because nobody remembered my birthday, and now to sulk all evening because nobody would spend my birthday party helping me work a case.

As we were going back to our cars after dinner, Olead cornered me in the parking lot. "Deb," he said, "don't worry."

"About what?"

"About anything. Don't worry, do you hear me? I mean it. Don't worry." He grinned. "Here's your birthday card."

"You already gave me a birthday card."

"So here's another one." He stuck it into my hand. "Read it at home."

I figured out what he meant after we had dropped Lori off at her house, got home, and sent Hal to bed. After Harry returned from seeing May Rector to her front door, he came into the bedroom where I was wandering about clad in a towel, just having emerged from the shower, and said, "I want to show you something."

He handed me the bank statement.

"I'll look at the bank statement later," I protested, "It's the middle of the night and I have to—Oh. Oh my gosh." Despite my protests, my eyes had followed his pointing finger to a deposit—a twenty-thousand dollar deposit. "That's a heck of a mistake," I said feebly. "Usually mistakes are in the bank's favor."

"I called the bank. It isn't a mistake. The teller said she'd never seen that much cash at one time in her life. She said the deposit was made by a tall man in his midtwenties, with brown hair and blue eyes."

"Olead," I said.

"Olead," he agreed. "Deb, I don't know what to do about it. I found it out about three this afternoon, and there hasn't been any time to talk about it since."

I reached for my purse, got out the second birthday card I'd forgotten till that moment, and opened it.

It wasn't a birthday card. It was a friendship card of sorts; the front cover was an elephant carrying a bunch of balloons in its trunk. The balloons informed me that elephants never forget. Inside, in Olead's handwriting, was a short note:

Deb—

You and Susan between you gave me back my life. Words cannot express my feelings. I can't give you anything like what you gave me. But some things I do have. Tell Harry it's okay. I just can't stand here and watch the two of you worrying yourselves sick over something I can help with this easily. Harry kept saying no and I could think of only one thing to do, so I did it. Don't argue.

Love,
Olead

Harry scratched his nose. "Well," he said.

"Harry, I didn't do anything much," I said. "I knew from the start he hadn't killed anybody. I couldn't just sit there and watch him get executed."

"Of course not," Harry said.

"So what are you going to do?" I asked. "About this?"

He scratched his nose again. "I guess I'm going to go pay bills. You get some sleep. *Hal, if you don't turn off that damn stereo I'm going to take it away from you. It's the middle of the night and your mother has to go to work in the morning!*"

"I'm turning if off," Hal yelled back, in tones of injured innocence, and the dulcet tones of Led Zeppelin or whatever it was this time ceased to waft out into the night.

WHEN I WOKE UP, Harry was still in the living room staring at a turned-off ham radio.

I planned to go see Brad that morning. At least, that was my intention. But I got a telephone call at seven o'clock. Matilda Greenwood had reported a murder.

It took me a minute to remember that Matilda Greenwood was Sister Eagle Feather.

FIVE

MATILDA GREENWOOD, in buckskin and beads instead of jeans and a sweatshirt, looked somewhat different from the way I had seen her the previous day. Her face was the same, of course, and so were the glossy black shoulder-length braids, but that was about all. She looked frightened, apprehensive, and pale, with a thin white line at the edge of her lips. I had seen people look like that before, usually when they were just about to pass out cold.

I had come to the scene directly from home, not bothering to go into the station first to get a police car, and I still didn't know any more about what was going on than what the dispatcher had told me over the telephone: a middle-aged woman, dead in bed, covers up to her neck.

Normally we would have treated that as a found body. Photograph, check medical record, and send to a funeral home. After yesterday, it called for the Major Case Squad. If that was a mistake, it was better to err on the side of caution.

I sat down on the couch, which I should not have done until after Irene Loukas told me I could, and said to Matilda, "You want to come tell me about it?"

She looked at me, startled, as if trying to decide whether to tell me or run away. Then she came over and sat down beside me, the pinched look slowly fading from her face. She wasn't going to faint right now. "Tell you what? I mean, you're the police..."

"Just one of them. And I just got here. I really don't know much about what's going on. What was her name?"

"Corie Meeks." Matilda brushed at her forehead as if a stray hair were getting in her way.

"How'd you happen to find her?"

"She called me last night about eleven-thirty. I'd already gone to bed—I go to bed pretty early most of the time. She was upset. She wanted me to come right over. I told her I was half asleep and couldn't she wait till morning. She said she'd cry all night. I said that was a shame, but I was too sleepy to be driving. So finally she said come about six-thirty in the morning. I get up pretty early, so that was okay, and I said I would."

"Is she a member of your church?"

Matilda laughed shortly. "There's something I guess I better explain."

I waited.

She fidgeted.

"I started out a psychologist," she said finally. "I mean, I've got a master's degree in clinical psychology."

I literally did not know what to say. I just sat there with my mouth open. Finally I managed to get out, "Then why Sister Eagle Feather?"

"It's all these depressed old ladies," she said. "They're the ones I wanted to help. But they won't go to psychologists or psychiatrists, or even tell their medical doctors they're depressed, even if they fill the doctors' offices with all kinds of vague complaints. But they flock to the charlatans. So I thought if I dressed up like a charlatan—and I really am a medium, even if you don't believe in it—I could reach them and help them maybe when nobody else could. At least I could protect them from the real charlatans. And if I could treat depression and make it look like mumbo jumbo...well, then they wouldn't have to feel embarrassed about depression... You know, so many older people act like any kind of emotional problem is a sin..." She floundered to a stop. Then she nodded. "Yes. Corie Meeks was in my church. But you know what else?"

"What else?"

"She's a secretary to a psychiatrist. You'd think she'd have better sense than to go to... to Sister Eagle Feather."

"What psychiatrist?" I asked, thinking that with all the coincidences that were going on I wouldn't be surprised if she said Brad Graves.

But she didn't. She said Corie was secretary to Dr. Samuel Barrett.

I didn't know Samuel Barrett—not that there was any reason why I should. I certainly don't know every psychiatrist in town. "Has anybody notified Dr. Barrett?" I asked.

Matilda shook her head. "I don't know. I haven't. I doubt if anybody has. Not yet."

Irene Loukas bustled into the living room and stopped short. "Deb," she said in an awful voice, "what do you think you're doing?"

"Talking with a possible witness. Did you have a nice vacation?"

"I got a wisdom tooth out."

"For that you take sick leave, not vacation," I told her.

She ignored me. "Did I tell you I was ready to release that couch?"

"No, you did not," I said meekly, "but you're not going to get fingerprints off—"

"Did you ever hear of fiber?"

Yes, I had "ever" heard of fiber. The theory is that every time one piece of fiber touches another, there is fiber transfer. What this means is that if a man in blue jeans sits down on a red couch, theoretically when he gets up he'll take microscopic red fibers away on his jeans, and he'll leave microscopic blue fibers on the couch. Two-thirds of the time this theory doesn't work out in practice—not that the fibers aren't there, but if they are there (and they probably are) they're too minute to be found with anything we have to work with.

The one-third of the time fiber transfer really does verifiably occur, the results can be pretty weird. In other areas besides criminology. One book I read on the Shroud of Turin said that among the identified fibers clinging to the shroud, obviously put there by fiber transfer, was one fragment of a pink cloth that had never been used for anything except women's girdles. I told Harry it boggles the mind to try to figure out how a fiber from a pink girdle got on the Shroud of Turin.

Most of the fibers that turn up in the kind of work Irene was doing have as much to do with the crime as the pink girdle fiber has to do with the authenticity of the Shroud of Turin.

Anyway, Irene was mad at me because, theoretically, if whoever killed Corie Meeks—assuming Corie Meeks had been killed, which as of now we had no reason to assume—had sat down on the couch, then the couch would now bear minute fibers from his or her clothing, which Matilda and I would now have tampered with and, quite possibly, be carrying away on our clothing, leaving behind... Oh well, you get the picture.

I would not meddle with anything that might hold fingerprints. But I felt the likelihood of any real evidence coming off this couch was so small as to be negligible. And Matilda had looked as if she needed to sit down.

Irene, offended, headed back into another room, and I returned my attention to Matilda. "Okay, so Corie asked you to get here at six-thirty in the morning and you did, right?"

Matilda nodded.

"So how do we get from there to finding the body?"

"They think I did it, don't they?" Matilda asked.

"Nobody thinks anything yet. We don't have any evidence to reason from. That's why I'm talking to you. Of course, if you don't want to talk to me, or if you'd rather call a lawyer first—"

"Never mind," Matilda said. She clasped her hands together oddly, both arms stretched out in front of her with the backs of her forearms touching each other, her wrists intertwined. In that position, she leaned forward and stretched.

"What are you doing?" I asked.

"Stretching. Why?"

"I thought you might be doing yoga or something. I never saw anybody in that position before."

"Just stretching. Okay. I got here at six-thirty. You've noticed how the place is laid out?"

I nodded. It was a ground-floor apartment, adjoined to other apartments on both sides. The front door opened onto a sidewalk, which led through the grassy front yard to the street, and there were two front ground-floor windows, both in the living room, one on either side of the door. A large back window and a back door opened onto a brick-walled private patio, which led in turn to the carports. The door leading out of the patio into the parking area was securely padlocked. Although I had not tried to open the front windows, they looked as if they had been painted shut. Which meant that Sister Eagle Feather—and the killer, if killer there was and if it wasn't Sister Eagle Feather—had entered through the front door and, at least in the case of the killer, exited that way.

"So I got here—that's my car parked out in front— and I came to the door and rang the doorbell. She didn't answer, and then I noticed the door was standing open—not much, just two or three inches—and so I thought maybe she had gotten up and opened the door for me and then gone back to bed or gone to take a shower. So I stepped inside, you know how you do, and called 'Corie?' I didn't hear anything, and the place was dark. So I was rather annoyed . . . to call me out like this and not even be awake . . . So I went into her bedroom—"

"You knew where it was?"

"Oh, yes. Corie is—was—always needing her hand held. She needed more help than I could give her. But I stepped into the bedroom and turned the light on. I was going to wake her up. And then . . . I saw her."

"You touched her?"

"I didn't need to touch her. I saw her. And then I went in the other room and called the police."

"Exactly what did you see?"

"She was lying on her back with the covers up to her chin. Her . . . let me think . . . her right arm was hanging off the bed, and the fingers had this weird bluish color. You know what I mean?"

That wasn't a verbal tic, as "you know what I mean" so often is. It was a question. I nodded. I knew what she meant. It is called postmortem lividity, and it begins to develop immediately after death, much sooner than rigor mortis. "I know what you mean," I said. "Go on."

"Okay, well, and I saw her face. Her eyes were half open—not all the way open, but half open—and they had this dull look to them. I looked at all that, and her not moving. And I knew. I didn't have to touch her to know she was dead. I didn't have to, and I didn't want to, and I didn't."

"You've been here before." It wasn't a question, but Matilda nodded. "This morning, did you see anything other than the body that looked in any way unusual?"

"No," Matilda said. "And I looked. I walked around and looked, while I was waiting for the police to get here. Deb, I'm scared. Not about me, but...do you realize that's two people in my church in two days? I keep wondering, is it somebody from my church doing it? And legally I don't think I'm supposed to give you my membership rolls, but I think maybe I ought to anyway, but ethically...I don't know what to do!"

I didn't know what to do either. I've never had occasion to get a court order to look at church records, and I wasn't sure whether I could get such a court order. Even in reasonably conservative Fort Worth, Texas, with the church a spiritualist church that even its owner or founder or whatever you wanted to call her admitted wasn't really a church at all, I wasn't sure a judge would want to sign that kind of order.

I decided to leave that subject for now. "When Corie called you last night, did she tell you why?"

"No," Matilda said. "I told you she was always wanting her hand to be held. And she paid well for the privilege, though to be honest, I'd rather she'd taken her money elsewhere. I told her one time she needed a psychiatrist, and she was furious. I do know she had been engaged and the engagement was broken off... She said he'd found somebody richer to marry, but I don't know if that was true. She was always overdramatizing everything."

"Did she tell you her fiancé's name?"

"Uh-uh. No. No, she never did tell me that. And I wondered if there really was one at all, or if she was just . . . making it up."

"Did she make things up?"

"Oh, yes. She was always making things up. But that . . . I'm not sure. Deb, can I go home now?"

"You might as well." I could hear Dr. Habib on the steps outside, talking with a patrol officer. "I'll need a written statement, but I can get with you later about that. What I'd like you to do is this: as soon as you get home, sit down at your typewriter or word processor and write out everything you can think of about this morning, and about what Corie said last night, and anything else she might have told you."

Matilda murmured something about confidentiality, and I said impatiently, "She's dead. Is confidentiality all that important now?"

"It has to be," Matilda said. "She has a right to her privacy even if she is dead."

I didn't feel up to arguing about that right now. "Then write down anything you can that you don't think breaches confidentiality."

I saw her out the door. Habib and Davisson, the latter looking rather unhappy, entered, followed by Gil Sanchez, complete with camera and evidence kit. As usual, we were duplicating effort; Sanchez would redo everything Irene had already done except for collecting the evidence Irene had already collected and doing the fingerprinting Irene had already done.

I stood back and watched, as Sanchez took pictures and Habib *hmmed,* nodded two or three times, called Davisson (who was still looking unhappy), and pointed at something. I wasn't close enough to tell what. Habib in a demonstrative mood is—how shall I say it?—interesting. Once during an autopsy, he decided for no apparent reason that I could ever figure out to remove the entire digestive tract of the victim, lay it out beside the body, and explain to me its workings. In very great detail. It was interesting, but I still don't exactly know why he did it. It would have made sense if she'd been poisoned, but she'd died from a bad crack on the head. For quite a while after that I couldn't stop mentally tracing the entire course of every bite of food I ate.

He was still pointing things out to Davisson. Finally he turned and informed Sanchez that the body could be moved.

"You mind telling me what's going on?" I asked, only a little bit sarcastically. "After all, it is my case."

"Oh, yes, well, I don't want to say for sure until I've opened it up." Bodies become "it" to Habib, unless of course it happens to be a body he knew when it was alive, in which case he is very unhappy.

"You got any ideas at all?" I was quite sure he did.

"Well, yes, a few. I think we're going to find, in your words, a broken neck."

Those were his words, too. Exactly his words, when he was on the telephone yelling at me about Jane Stevenson. He becomes less scientific when he's angry. But, of course when he made an official written report it would be in medicalese that I would be unable to interpret without a dictionary.

And if he thinks he's going to find a broken neck, he's going to find a broken neck. Andrew Habib knows his business. So this was murder, and we were very fortunate indeed that an alert patrol officer, first on the scene, had spotted the similarity to Jane Stevenson, so that the case had been treated as murder from the start.

Irene had already photographed the body and fingerprinted everything in its immediate vicinity. Habib ordered "it" removed, and most of the assorted officialdom went with or shortly after it. That left only Irene and me indoors and a patrol officer on the front steps to make sure no unauthorized person entered the scene.

Irene and I started searching. As is my habit at crime scenes, I kept my hands clasped behind my back, so that I wouldn't absentmindedly touch something it wasn't yet time to touch. I let Irene move furniture slightly, lift draperies to look under their edges.

For all the good it didn't do. There was no sign whatever of violence. No drop of blood on the bathroom floor this time, no broken eyeglasses under the hem of the draperies. Nothing. If we were to judge by the scene, Corie Meeks had died peacefully, alone, in bed.

Which wasn't what happened.

We could deduce from Corie Meeks's books that she was interested in spiritualism, except that we didn't have to deduce it, because we already knew it. We could deduce that she had a cat. The cat wasn't in evidence—no surprise there, considering that the front door had been left partway open probably from the time the killer departed—but the cat's food, water, and litter box were visible. The litter had been changed since the last time the cat had used it. Knowing the habits of cats—they can't stand an unmarred surface on their litter—and knowing the habits of this killer at least well enough to know he (she?) cleaned up after the killing, I couldn't help wondering if the killer had changed the litter box.

I told myself that was perfectly ridiculous. But I also suggested Irene might dust the plastic of the litter box for prints, and take in the litter bag for ninhydrin testing. I'd rather look ridiculous than miss out on evidence.

I left Irene dusting for fingerprints and finding only scrub marks where somebody had washed or waxed everything in sight, and I went to talk with neighbors.

There was nobody home on the right. There was nobody home on the left.

Probably there'd be nobody home in this entire apartment complex except the resident manager. This was the kind of place where people went to work in the morning and came home at night to sleep.

A sign on the lawn said OFFICE L-4. RESIDENT MANAGER G-5.

The office was locked, and the sign on the front informed me it opened at ten. I proceeded, with some detouring because I didn't know the way, to G-5, which was an upstairs apartment back-to-back with D-4, where Corie Meeks lived. I rang the doorbell, and I rang the doorbell. An angry female voice inside, called, "*Now* what?"

"Police," I replied.

A brief scurry. The front door opened. Clutching a print cotton robe around her, she stared out at me from under tangled hair. "What is it?" she demanded, her tone resentful. "The baby howled all night, and what time he wasn't howling that idiot Corie Meeks played games with her light switch, and I'm half dead. I'm not open till ten. Can't you come back then?"

"I'm sorry to disturb you," I said. "I have a baby, too, so I know just how you feel. But I'm afraid I need to talk with you now. Corie Meeks has been murdered."

She stared at me, what color she had left draining from her cheeks. "What are you talking about? She can't be... You're not serious, are you? Murdered?"

"Yes, and I'd like to know more about her lights. You might have seen something—"

"Who are you?"

"Deb Ralston, Fort Worth Police Department." I produced identification. "I'd better get your name, too."

"Sue. Sue Jarvis. You want to know what I saw? Not anything, really. Just the lights. Look, you can see the way these places are laid out. Our bedrooms overlook her bedroom. Her light stayed on just forever last night. I guess it went off about three o'clock in the morning, and then it stayed off about ten minutes, and then it went off and on, off and on, off and on, like a little kid playing with the switch."

"How long did that go on?"

"I don't know. Maybe ten or twenty minutes. It felt like forever, with us trying to sleep."

"Did you see anything else?"

"I told you I didn't."

"Or hear..."

From somewhere behind her, a baby began to cry. He cried very loudly, and she gestured resignedly in that direction. "Over that? I told you he cried nearly all night. Come on in."

I followed her and waited as she checked the baby's diaper and got a bottle out of the refrigerator to heat. Only after the baby had quieted down with the bottle did I try to ask any more questions. By this time the manager, too, seemed calmer. "Did Corie have visitors very often?"

"That Indian woman. She usually came at night, but sometimes in the morning. Two or three men, but I never really noticed them, you know, not to say I noticed them, just that they were men. She had parties sometimes, and I had to warn her about making sure they used guest parking, because a time or two they took up all the parking and the other tenants were really mad when they couldn't get into their own spaces. I mean, the spaces are all numbered, and they're supposed to be reserved for the tenants in those particular apartments. It was pretty inconsiderate for visitors to take them. You'd think they'd realize if there were numbered spaces, then they were numbered for a reason. Oh, well, she was yelling at somebody about midnight, but I figured that was her ex-fiancé. It quit after a while."

"Did you know her ex-fiancé?"

"'No, she was real mysterious about him. And that was kind of funny because she talked so much about everything else. I mean, really, you never saw a person who talked as much as she did.''

"After the quarrel last night—"

"Oh, it wasn't a quarrel, just Corie yelling. I couldn't hear anything else."

"All right, well, after Corie got through yelling, did you see anybody leave?"

"At midnight? Anyway, I wouldn't have noticed. I can't see her front door from here, just her bedroom windows."

"Did you see anybody walking around there?"

"I wasn't looking. It was just that her light kept getting in my eyes."

This was not the most satisfactory witness I had ever talked with. Not that I blamed her for that; she'd obviously been busy with her own problems, and she'd had no reason at all to suspect anything was wrong at Corie's apartment. "Those parties," I said. "Were they always the same night?"

"Always. Wednesday night. That was kind of funny, you'd think she'd have them on Friday or Saturday night, when most people have parties, but..."

"Can you tell me a little about the parties? The kind of people who came to them? Were they loud parties?"

"Oh, no, they were real quiet. I wouldn't have minded a bit if it hadn't been for the parking. I don't know, maybe a dozen people, twenty people, something like that. Men and women both. Not real dressed up, just normal dress. Shorts, slacks, T-shirts. There was this one guy I couldn't help noticing because he had this, like it was a baseball cap, only it had a fox's face, all furry and everything, on it. No drinking at all that I noticed, no loud music . . . none of the kinds of things people usually do at parties. They almost seemed more like meetings than parties, except sometimes you could hear them all laughing, and anyway I don't know what kind of meetings she would have been having."

I didn't like the hunch I was having. "Could I borrow your phone?" I asked.

"Yeah, sure, it's in the living room."

Susan wasn't with patients, yet. That was fortunate; it meant I could talk with her at once instead of having to chase her through appointments and ask her to call me back and then not know where I was going to be so she could call me back.

"Yes, I know Corie Meeks," she said cautiously, when I asked her. "Why?"

I told her.

There was a long silence at Susan's end of the phone. Then she said, "Why did you call me?"

I told her about the parties. "Yes, they were Mensa SIG meetings," she said. "The same group. We met over here sometimes, too. Brad's apartment. Several other places."

"What can you tell me about Corie?"

Another long silence. "She's... she was... a very strange woman. Really odd."

"Strange in what way?"

Still more silence. "I have to go, Deb, I have an appointment. Anyway, I can't tell you anything else."

"Can't or won't?" I had run into the stone wall of Susan's professional sensibilities before. But I didn't think that was what I was meeting here, not with this impenetrable barrier of silence that met every question, including this one. Finally she said, "I have to go now." And she did.

I didn't have anything else to ask Sue Jarvis, not really. Besides that, it was nearly ten, and she still had to comb her hair and dress before opening the office. I went to try to talk to more neighbors.

This time I got a man across the street—actually, the driveway through the apartment complex—from Corie. Jack Tatum didn't know Corie particularly well, only by sight and barely that. But he worked nights (luckily I caught him after he got up, so he wasn't in too bad a mood) and he'd gotten home last night at one A.M. to find his parking spot occupied. He was mildly annoyed, but reminded himself that if he let himself get upset it would disturb his sleep, and wouldn't hurt the parking place pirate (that was his phrase) in the slightest. So he went and parked in the guest area, walked back to his apartment, and went to bed.

"What did it look like, the car in your spot?" I asked.

He shook his head. "You know how those yellow lights distort color. All I can tell you is, it was a sedan. Light color. Not real old but not new enough it still had the dealer's sticker in the window."

"I don't suppose you happened to notice the license plate?"

"You suppose right. I didn't. Look, it was one o'clock in the morning. All I wanted to do was go to bed. For all the good it did. That damned cat kept yowling outside my window for another couple of hours, and I didn't really get settled down until it shut up."

"What cat was that?"

He stared at me. "Corie Meeks's cat, of course. Pets aren't allowed in this complex, but she managed to pull strings somehow or else she just doesn't—didn't— care about the rules, because she had this big ole Siamese tomcat. And I guess he was hunting romance last night, because he sat outside my window...oh, actually, I guess he was out in the street somewhere, but it sounded like he was just outside my window...and he yowled and he howled, and he howled and he yowled. Finally shut up about three o'clock in the morning.''

Three o'clock in the morning. Sue Jarvis said Corie Meeks's light had gone off about that time. Now Jack Tatum said Corie Meeks's cat had stopped yowling about that time. Could there be any connection?

It didn't make sense that there could be. Especially since Sue Jarvis had also said that Corie's light had gone off and on, off and on, for another ten to twenty minutes after that—which didn't make sense either. What killer would want to call attention to himself that way? Unless he wanted to get caught.

Anyway, where *was* the missing cat? I hadn't thought much about it earlier, seeing the pet dishes and the litter box. Obviously, I had no way of knowing where it was.

What I did know was that it was nearly eleven o'clock in the morning and both the breakfast I had never had and the lunch that was coming due soon were calling me loudly. In fact, I was hungry to the point of giddiness—not actual dizziness, but I could feel silliness coming on. I would head back over to Corie's apartment, check in with Irene to see if she was going to be much longer and if she wanted me to bring her anything to eat, and then I'd head on out.

On my way back to the apartment, I was waylaid by a middle-aged woman. A woman about my own age, that is to say, but with a new (well, fairly new) baby, I find it hard to convince myself I'm really middle-aged. "Are you the police?" she demanded.

"One of them, anyway. Deb Ralston. Why?"

"Oh, I just wanted to know what was going on over at Corie's place. You know, I went to go in, and there was this policeman at the door and he wouldn't let me in, and when I asked him if something was wrong with Corie he said 'Police business, ma'am,' and wouldn't tell me anything, and she's about my best friend, and somebody ought to tell me—"

"Is there any reason why something should be wrong with Corie?" I asked cautiously.

"Well, you know, she's been real despondent, that boyfriend tossing her over the way he did, and I thought maybe she might've, you know, well..."

"No, that's not what happened," I said. "Do you live near here?"

"Right over there." She pointed.

Of course I was taking this "best friend" business with a grain of salt—police in the neighborhood bring out a lot of "best friends" who are really no more than nosy neighbors—but all the same, if this woman, whoever she was, really was a good friend of Corie Meeks, she ought to have a little privacy before she heard what had happened.

I talked her into leading me over to her apartment, and got her name out of her. It was Genny Cantrell,

Genny being short for Genevieve, not Virginia or Jennifer. (I asked.)

I talked her into sitting down and then told her what had happened. She cried a little bit, but not enough for me to believe that she was really Corie's closest friend, and then she started asking questions, most of which I could not answer and the rest of which I had no business answering.

I managed to fend her off and ask questions of my own.

As I suspected, she had never met Corie's fiancé and had never heard him called by name. But all the same she was sure it was Corie's fiancé who had killed her.

In which suspicion she might have been right. But she might also have been wrong.

Leaving her torn between mourning and excitement, I returned to Corie's apartment to find Irene sitting on the bedroom floor dusting the biggest pile of vodka bottles I had ever seen outside of a bar. "What in the world?" I demanded.

Irene gestured at the dresser drawer she was sitting beside. I looked. Even without the bottles she had already dragged out, the drawer was over half full of vodka bottles. All Prince Ivan brand—which I had been informed is not a very good brand, though not being a vodka drinker myself I wouldn't know—and all empty.

Disentangling herself from the vodka bottles, Irene stood up and flung open the lid of a cedar chest that sat at the foot of the bed. I looked. It also was half full of vodka bottles, also Prince Ivan, also empty. The rest of the cedar chest contained sweaters and knitting yarn. I knew it was knitting yarn, not crochet yarn, because the knitting needles and an assortment of knitting patterns were tucked in with it.

Irene opened another dresser drawer. It too contained vodka bottles, same brand, full ones this time, along with a small assortment of underwear and a framed photograph of which I could see only the back. "Okay if I touch?" I asked.

Irene nodded.

I turned it over.

The glass was cracked, but not so severely cracked that I couldn't recognize a studio portrait of Bradley Graves.

SIX

As I drove toward Bradley Graves's office, let us say that I did not find myself in the greatest mood I have ever enjoyed in my whole entire life. I was thinking of patterns. Shapes of things. Shapes of events.

I had two dead women, Jane Stevenson and Corie Meeks. Both knew Brad Graves. Well, I conscientiously reminded myself that was because both belonged, as unlikely as it might seem, to the same Mensa chapter that Brad Graves belonged to. So that wasn't necessarily a suspicious circumstance. But one of them had apparently been engaged to him, an engagement that had been broken off, and she had a studio portrait of him in her apartment. And nobody goes around handing out studio portraits to everybody he knows. Nobody except actors and people like that, anyway.

There were, of course, other connections the women had in common. They did both belong to that same Mensa chapter, and obviously I needed to find out, if anybody would tell me, the names of everybody in that chapter. And they both belonged to Sister Eagle Feather's spiritualist church, but after the time I'd spent with Matilda Greenwood, I was less inclined than I had been to find that suspicious. All the same, I needed to get the church rolls if I could.

And I needed to find out, fast, how many members of the SIG group, and how many members of Matilda's church, were older women living alone. Find out and warn them. Before nightfall.

Normally, when you have two or more similar killings, you start to look for connections between the victims, similarities shared by the victims. Normally those connections, those similarities, help lead you to a suspect. But this time I had too many connections, too many similarities.

I didn't like that. And what I liked even less was the fact that Brad Graves, who was a tentative suspect whether or not he had ever been engaged to marry Corie Meeks, was now engaged to marry my closest friend.

Dr. Graves had his office in an upper site in one of the Tandy Center buildings. Towers, they actually are, and I have frequently wondered why they are not called Tandy Towers instead of Tandy Center. But mine is not to reason why, and so forth. The location suggested he had plenty of money, but it struck me as a rather odd place to have a psychiatrist's office. But here, as in other areas, my knowledge was perhaps more limited than I would like to admit.

No, I did not park in the Tandy parking lot and take the Tandy subway under the river to get there. I parked in the police station parking lot, which is only a couple of blocks away from the Tandy Center, and walked. True, that isn't the nicest neighborhood in the world, but then, I was armed. My pistol wasn't in my purse, which can be snatched from a police officer as easily as it can from any other woman, but rather in the shoulder holster I have been wearing very nearly as long as I have been in plain clothes.

As usual, people were ice skating on the ice rink—funny as that sounds in Fort Worth, Texas—in the middle of the ground floor. As usual, all the little stores were having sidewalk sales and otherwise luring customers in. As usual, enticing smells—extremely enticing, considering that I still had not eaten—were floating out of the restaurants, and the escalators that supplied the shopping mall part of the building were crowded.

This time I didn't take the escalator. I went to the bank of elevators that supplied the upper parts of the building. Twelfth floor. He was on the twelfth floor.

In a couple of minutes, I was explaining to the nurse or receptionist or whatever she was that, no, I did not have an appointment with Dr. Graves, but I was a police officer and I intended to see him with or without an appointment.

"He's with a patient," the nurse or receptionist or whatever she was said, in that precise, high-pitched voice medical people tend to use when they are talking to people who are slightly retarded, drunk, or otherwise incapacitated. "I really can't interrupt him. It could be very harmful to the patient."

That was probably true. I didn't have an arrest warrant or a search warrant, so I couldn't just barge in anyway. "When will he be through with the patient?" I asked, probably sounding as grumpy as I felt.

"This patient's hour is up at one o'clock," she said, "and after that Dr. Graves is going to lunch."

"Good," I said. "Tell him Deb Ralston will be joining him for lunch on official business."

"Ms. Ralston," whoever she was (I wished to goodness she had a nameplate in front of her or a pin with her name on it) asked stuffily, "does Dr. Graves know you?"

"Dr. Graves knows me," I was able to reassure her, "and he was expecting me. He just didn't know when I was coming. I'll be back at one."

I glanced at my watch as I went back out the door. Twelve-oh-five. I must have gone in his door about two seconds after he closeted himself with the patient. That meant I had about forty-five minutes to kill, as I intended to be back by ten minutes till one. One thing I had learned from Susan was that psychiatrists' hours with their patients tend to be closer to fifty minutes. Sometimes even forty-five. Well, that makes sense. Everybody needs a break now and then, if only to go to the bathroom and get a drink of water.

I wondered if Dr. Graves was the kind of psychiatrist who had his patients lie down on a couch to talk. I wondered if that kind of psychiatrist even existed anymore. Never having had the occasion for a professional visit with a psychiatrist, I had no way of knowing unless I asked, and I didn't expect I was going to.

Tandy Center is replete with tunnels and skyways. Not only does it have the subway tunnel under the Trinity River—I have been told that is the longest private subway in the world, though frankly, I doubt that's true—but it also has skyways from one of the towers to the other, and to the other adjoining luxury hotel. It even has a tunnel that goes under the street and leads into the public library. Among other things, that means that if the library parking lot is full, which it often is, you can park across the river in the spacious Tandy parking lot, take the subway under the river—at least I guess it's under the river; I've been told that, but I've never actually checked for myself—to the Tandy Center, and then walk down the nice, well-lighted tunnel right into the library. The place is patrolled not only by Fort Worth police officers but also by Tandy security guards, so that you are actually safer than you would be on the street.

I didn't exactly know why I was going to the library. My subconscious probably had a reason that had not yet filtered through to my conscious mind. Minds seem to work like that, or at least mine does.

Inside, I found the reference section and asked the librarian if there was some kind of book that listed all the doctors in the county with their qualifications. I still didn't know what I was looking for. Clearly, I was on a fishing expedition, and I'd figure out what kind of fish I was fishing for if I happened to get a bite.

"Well, not in the *county*," she said.

"What, then?" I asked.

She found me a book that listed doctors from all over the state, with their qualifications. I looked up Bradley Graves and found nothing that looked at all out-of-the-way to me. For extra measure, I looked up Samuel Barrett, our newest corpse's employer, and also found nothing out-of-the-way. I still didn't know what I was looking for, and I still had thirty minutes to kill, so I amused myself by looking up all the doctors I knew. Outside of finding out that a doctor I met at the Kerrville Folk Festival—she is tall and slim, has black hair that hangs down to her waist, prefers to wear the legal minimum of clothing when she is not on duty, and everybody calls her J.P.—actually had the unlikely (for her) first name of Joanne. I found nothing at all of interest.

I still didn't know what I had expected to find.

Ignoring the sign that said DO NOT RESHELVE BOOKS, I stuck the book back on the shelf and went back to ask the reference librarian about spiritualism. She told me that would be in the same general area as books on religion and asked if I needed help again. I didn't. I went to look. Grabbing a couple of books more or less at random, I headed for the checkout desk, meeting there a library clerk who has eyed my purse with great interest ever since the day I was checking out a couple of romances (all right, laugh) and opened my purse to reveal the unlikely juxtaposition of a baby bottle and a pistol.

She seemed disappointed that neither was in evidence this time.

As I was now on the upper level (there is a checkout counter at the library entrance to the tunnel, but there's hardly ever anybody working at it), I jaywalked across the street and went back to the Tandy Center, entering on the second level. I could have leaned over the rail and watched the ice-skaters below if I had any inclination to do that, which as it happened I did not.

Sitting down in the psychiatric waiting room, I began to read one of the books. It seemed to have absolutely nothing to do with Sister Eagle Feather. I learned far more than I ever wanted to know about a couple of sisters who eventually admitted to fraud in the case of an apparent intelligent poltergeist that claimed to be the spirit of a peddler who had been murdered and buried in the wall of the cellar in the house the girls now lived in. Their confession had been thrown into considerable question later when a skeleton was unearthed from the cellar, with a peddler's pack walled in beside it.

Hmm, I thought, reflecting on false confessions. Every police officer gets plenty of those, even when not afflicted with the Ed Goughs of the world, and just about every large city has at least one Ed Gough who runs in to confess to murders he hasn't committed. Let's see, it was now October, and so far I had had Ed in my office at least twenty times since the beginning of the year, and that doesn't even count the months I was out on maternity leave. He confessed to one or two of the bank teller murders, and then there was that missing teenager whose murder he confessed to. She turned out not to have been murdered at all, or even to be really missing. She'd merely gone camping with her grandparents. She'd told her mother before she left, but the mother was sound asleep, and what the teenager interpreted as consent was only that vague "uh-huh" mothers, and sometimes fathers, make when semiawakened by an importunate child with whom they do not wish to interact until much later in the morning.

A young woman with downcast eyes came out past the receptionist-or-whatever's desk, and the receptionist-or-whatever went in the same door. A couple of minutes later Brad Graves came out. "Hi, Deb, sorry you had to wait," he said cheerfully.

"Oh, well, you didn't know when I was coming. I don't really need to go to lunch with you, of course, I just want to ask a few—"

"Well, *I* have to go to lunch. I have another appointment at one-thirty. So you might as well join me."

I do not enjoy sharing a meal with somebody I at least halfway suspect of murder. All the same, I have done it before. He headed for a restaurant inside Tandy Center—this must be convenient in bad weather—where they do a nice spinach salad I like. It wasn't until we were seated upstairs where it was quieter (the downstairs is actually more of a bar than a restaurant) that he said, "Now. You wanted to ask about Jane Stevenson."

"Well, I do," I said, "but first I want to ask about Corie Meeks."

"Corie Meeks?" He stopped in the act of unfolding a maroon linen napkin to stare at me sharply. "What about Corie Meeks?"

"What do you know about her?"

He hesitated. "I'm afraid I'm not going to answer that unless you tell me why you're asking. After all, people do have a right to a certain amount of privacy. And surely you're not thinking Corie would have done anything to harm—"

"Corie is dead," I broke in abruptly. I was really getting sick of hearing about people's right to privacy.

"Dead." It was too flat to be an exclamation. "Corie Meeks is dead?" I nodded. "And from the fact that you're the one asking questions, I judge she was not exactly hit by a car."

"She was not hit by a car," I confirmed.

A long silence, during which a waiter approached the table to inquire what we would have to drink. Brad Graves was drinking club soda and lime juice. So was I. The waiter departed, and Brad said, "She was a pest. But not in the way that Jane was a pest."

"Go on," I said.

"Jane was a follower, a clinger. She had hitched herself up to some woman that ran a spiritualist church, and she'd gotten it in her head that emotional illness, mental illness, can be healed as easily by a shaman approach as by any kind of psychotherapy. In which, by the way, there is considerable evidence that she is right, but that's neither here nor there. She had decided she was going to become a healer, and she had joined our SIG so she could hang around with healers. Which is not a term I use—that's her term. I wish I thought I was a healer. A psychiatrist—or a psychologist, for that matter—doesn't heal. He helps the patient to heal himself, or herself, if possible. If that makes sense."

It made perfectly good sense to me; I'd heard somewhat the same thing from Susan often enough. "That's not necessarily accurate either," he added thoughtfully. "It's just... Look, the more we know about the interconnection of the mind, body, and emotions, the more we know we don't know. Sometimes what is manifesting itself as a mental illness is in fact a physical illness, and in that case, if we happen to know enough about that physical illness to do something about it, we can cure or at least treat it. Other times something that's really a mental illness is manifesting itself as a physical illness, and all the antibiotics and pain medication in the world won't do a bit of good until you get at the underlying problem. So the first problem in treating anything, ostensibly mental or emotional or physical, is to try to find out what the real problem is, and if you can do that more often than one time out of three you're a hell of a lot smarter than I am."

I was silent, thinking of my son-in-law Olead Baker, who had spent over ten years in a very expensive, very plush, but quite locked mental hospital with the diagnosis of schizophrenia, until his old doctor died and that doctor's daughter took over the hospital and found out that all that was ailing Olead was a severe vitamin B deficiency—which did not, Susan had assured both Olead and me, by any means prove that all, or even most, cases of apparent schizophrenia could be treated with vitamin B.

"But the point I'm trying to get to is that Jane somehow got it into her head that by hanging around with Sister White Owl or whatever her name was—"

"Sister Eagle Feather," I interposed.

"Whatever. Anyhow, Jane had got it into her head that by hanging around with her and with us, she was going to learn all the secrets of healing and become a healer herself, and then she would heal herself of that heart ailment nobody else could heal. She was dying of it, and a blind man could see that. And what made that really crazy was, we weren't having our meetings to talk about medicine."

"What were you doing?"

"As often as not, playing Trivial Pursuit."

The waiter brought our drinks. Brad immediately drained his and asked for a refill with lunch. He ordered a tuna salad plate. I ordered the spinach salad. He looked disapproving and informed me that it had egg in it.

"I know," I said.

"At your age, you ought to start thinking about cholesterol," he said.

"I know," I said, "I eat oat bread and I hardly ever eat anything but Cheerios for breakfast. But right now I want a spinach salad. Look, I get enough of this from Susan. She still says I need to gain weight."

"You look all right to me."

"I want to change the subject. Everybody always wants to doctor me, and I'm sick of it. You told me about Jane. Now what about Corie?"

He looked very uncomfortable. "I don't see how this can have anything to do with your investigation."

"Was she engaged to marry you?"

"Oh, hell," he said. "She thought she was. Look, Corie was unbalanced. Really unbalanced. Samuel Barrett—her employer—had told me several times he needed to get her out of the office, but he was afraid if he fired her she'd suicide. She was that unbalanced. And she... Look, I don't know how she got it in her head. I really do not know. I never even saw her away from the Mensa meetings, except one night when her car wouldn't start and I offered to take her home. But she decided we were going to get married. Well, it wasn't me she was after to start with, it was Sam. Her boss Sam is younger than I am, you see. But when Sam got married, she transferred the delusion—that's really all you can reasonably call it—to me. She used to call me at the office and tell Hallie, my receptionist, it was urgent. Hallie'd put her through, and she'd be planning her wedding dress. She'd call me at home and leave messages on my answering machine, and I couldn't change my phone number because my patients have to be able to get hold of me."

"So you're saying this engagement was a delusion?" If it was—and if in one part of her mind she knew it was—that would explain why, although she'd told everybody she knew she was engaged, she'd never told anybody who she was engaged to. That way she could call it off with less embarrassment to herself.

"A delusion, yes. A deliberate self-deception, I'm inclined to think."

"Was that nice studio portrait a delusion too?" That was what I had come to ask, mainly.

"I thought that was where it went," he said. "But I wasn't sure. I figured it was best to let her keep it, if she was the one who took it, and I couldn't think of anybody else who would have been likely to take it."

"You want to tell me about it?" I asked.

He nodded, and waited while the tuna plate was set in front of him. He started eating and half absent-mindedly talking around the food. "Yeah. I had . . . Look, Susan and I weren't ready to make any formal announcements yet because we had a lot to think about. Not just names—for professional reasons, she's about got to keep her own—but questions about her hospital, and my practice, and how to keep disruption to our patients to a minimum. We've been...talking around things, and then talking about things . . . for quite a few months."

He paused, looked a little embarrassed. "I asked her not to tell anybody—even you, and she really thinks the world of you—until we got it all thought out. But anyway, I had this studio portrait made to give to Susan. I hadn't given it to her yet. We had a Mensa meeting at my apartment, and after the meeting was over, well, Susan stayed late, and when she was ready to leave I was going to give her the portrait and I couldn't find it. Look, I'll admit I've been living alone quite a few years and I'm not exactly the tidiest fellow in the world, but I'm not so messy I could bring a framed picture home and lose it in the next four hours. So... I thought Corie must have taken it, because I couldn't think who else would have. I told Susan that and she agreed. We felt it wouldn't make sense to ask Corie to give it back, because either she'd deny having it or she might, well, get really upset. So I just called the photographer and asked to have another copy made, and I gave that to Susan, and we didn't worry about it anymore."

"So it didn't worry you that this demented woman might be going around showing off the picture and telling people she was going to marry you?"

He stared at me. "She wasn't demented. She was acting out her fantasies, but she certainly wasn't demented."

I did not get anything else out of him except my lunch, which he insisted on paying for. Obviously I needed to talk with Samuel Barrett sometime that day, if not the next. I mentioned that to Brad, and he said,

"Come on back to my office and I'll call and tell him you're coming."

Hallie, whose name and position I finally knew, was not in the office. Apparently she too had gone to lunch. But instead of using the phone at her desk, Brad called from an inside office. He took me with him, so that I could hear all of his end of the conversation, which I might have paid more attention to, if I had not been looking at a bar cart that contained, among other things, a bottle of Prince Ivan vodka.

He said, "Thanks," hung up, and then told me Sam was expecting me. Then he noticed the direction of my gaze and flushed slightly. "Habit I got into in my student days," he explained. "Cheap vodka. But they say with vodka you can't tell the difference. I certainly can't." I didn't reply, though I was certainly thinking fast, and he gave me directions to Barrett's office, which was located not too far from Hulen Mall. That's a part of town I hardly ever go to on my own, and I tend as a result to get lost when I'm over there on official business. Well, that's not the only reason, of course; the roads seem a lot more winding and curvy than they are in my part of town, where they go in more or less straight lines.

Dr. Sam Barrett was waiting for me. He was indeed younger than Brad, probably by at least fifteen years. He looked about thirty, which considering all a person goes through in order to get to be a psychiatrist is probably about as young as they come. He was nice looking, with black hair and eyebrows, blue eyes, and a very fair skin, the kind of face that looks vaguely Irish. Either he had two receptionists to start with, or else he'd lost no time in hiring a replacement or calling a temporary agency and having them send around a substitute. But he was waiting for me himself, which would be rather flattering if it were not for the fact that most likely he didn't want to have to explain to a receptionist, especially a temporary or newly hired one, what the police were doing coming to talk with him.

He took me straight back to an office with thick draperies, thick carpet floors, and sound-deadening ceiling tiles. "Now," he said, "Brad said you wanted to talk to me about Corie."

"Right. First, let me ask, are you also a member of Mensa?"

"Not eligible," he answered lightly. "I miss it by about half a point. I probably could bellow and yell and fudge a test or two and get in, but why bother?"

I looked at him in some dismay. This doctor with all these diplomas isn't eligible for Mensa, and Olead thinks *I* am?

"Was that all you wanted to ask me?" he prodded. He must be a different type of psychiatrist than Brad, I thought. Brad seems to work at making people comfortable; Samuel Barrett seemed to work at making people uncomfortable. Susan tried once to explain to me how many different types of psychiatrists there are, but I got a headache listening and she gave up.

"Did you know Jane Stevenson at all?" I asked.

"No, I didn't."

"Tell me about Corie Meeks."

He sighed. "This practice used to be a partnership," he said. "When I was ready to enter practice, I went to work for Ezra Loundes, and later he invited me to make it a partnership. Then Ezra . . . died." He didn't have to go into detail on that. I knew, and he knew I'd know. Dr. Ezra Loundes was shot in his front yard by a pair of teenagers who thought they'd find drugs in his house or car. We know that was the motive because they told us, later, after a patrol car answering a silent burglar alarm found Loundes dead in his front yard, found his wife—also Dr. Loundes— dead inside the house, found two teenagers tearing up the den hunting for the drugs they were convinced were present. Not that they needed any themselves; they were both stoned out of their minds on a combination of two or three different uppers and downers.

"So you kept the practice going," I said.

He nodded. "Yes. And I don't know if you knew Ezra."

"Not well. But I guess everybody in town knew him."

"Yeah. Everybody in town knew him. Him and his causes. Arrested at Glen Rose for protesting the nuclear power plant—"

"Actually he was arrested for cutting the fence," I pointed out. "He could have protested till hell froze over if he'd stayed on the outside of the fence."

"Ask the people in Chernobyl if the fallout stays on its side of the fence," Barrett challenged me.

"I'm not a decision maker," I said.

"Nobody is," Barrett replied. "Nobody is. And we're all going to sit on our decisionless little asses until the world blows up and our decisionless little asses are blown halfway to Mars. All right. Never mind. I try to be a worthy successor to Ezra. He had his causes. He had a screwed-up office because of his causes. He hired Corie because she needed the job, not because she could do the job, and the fact was she couldn't. Did you know one of those teens who shot him had worked for him."

"No, I didn't know that."

"Well, he did. Did yard work. Not because Ezra needed him. He didn't; he'd hired a big landscape firm, and they came in once a week and did anything that needed doing, from watering the lawn to replanting the flower beds. But the kid needed work so Ezra hired him, and nine days later he shot Ezra down in cold blood. But... he hired Corie. And I wasn't going to fire her. I just..." He looked embarrassed. "I wound up hiring somebody else to do the work. I let Corie sit and answer phones and half the time she got the messages wrong, but . . . Ezra hired her.''

''Okay. Brad said she wanted to marry you.''

''Well. That was another reason why I hired a second secretary, besides getting the work done. I . . . I didn't ever want to be alone with Corie Meeks. Not ever. If you know what I mean.''

''I think I know what you mean.''

''So I don't know what ever possessed Brad to offer to take her home. Her car was no more not running than the man in the moon. She went and got it the next day. It was running just fine.''

''So you think she pretended it was disabled so Brad would take her home.''

''I don't just think it, I know it. She told me, you know. She was telling everybody she knew that she was engaged, and I was the only one that she told who her 'fiancé' was. And I knew it wasn't true. I tried tactfully to point it out. She wasn't listening. Brad called me a couple of times to ask me how to discourage her. Hell, I don't—didn't—know. I told him you might could discourage her with a submachine gun, but I didn't know any other way.''

Might could. With that phrase, which he probably wouldn't have used if he'd been calmer, he'd betrayed his origins. Lower-class or lower-middle-class

Southern, most likely from East Texas. I was hearing a lot of East Texas in his accent.

"Thank you," I said. "I think you've answered all my questions."

Politely, he led me back to the front door. By now there was a patient waiting, looking somewhat peeved that somebody else was using part of his time. I thanked Barrett again and went back to my car. I still had my personal car, not having made time yet to go to the police station to get a detective car, though I had begged a walkie-talkie from somebody who was headed straight back to the station. I sat in the car now and thought.

If he'd stopped talking about one minute before he did, I'd have dismissed Brad Graves from all suspicion. But now I couldn't. What if Corie Meeks had been trying to blackmail Brad into marrying her? What if she had been threatening to say he'd assaulted her that night he took her home? Could his reputation stand the resulting publicity? Could anybody's?

And if a man—an intelligent man who felt seriously threatened, a man whose entire way of life, let alone his livelihood, was being endangered—if such a man decided murder was the only way out, how would he do it? Would he try to make it look like a hit-and-run, or would he try to make it look like a series of murders for which he would have no motive?

This would by no means be the first time that seemingly motiveless mass murder had been used as a mask for a personal kill. If that was the case, as it had been the case before...

My mind, never very disciplined, was wandering all over the place. The point I was trying to get myself to was this: When someone sets up an apparently un-motivated murder series to mask a personal kill, the personal kill isn't the first in the series, because even the stupidest killer would know that when the first kill happens we would look for a personal motive. It wouldn't be the last kill, because if the series stops abruptly immediately after someone for whom there is a motive, we'd know to look there. No, it would be the middle kill. In a series of three, it would be the second.

Which meant if this killer was Brad Graves, there would be a third kill.

Of whom?

Was that suave, debonair lady-killer literally a lady-killer? And did he really want to marry Susan Braun, who resembled nobody so much as Alice's White Queen? I could see Susan flying through the woods like the Queen, with her shawl trailing the ground and her hair falling down. In fact, I *had* once seen Susan with a beautiful white mohair crocheted shawl falling off her shoulders and her braids, as usual, falling down from their supposedly anchored position.

Susan would not appreciate a dithering telephone call from me.

Of course, I stopped at the next telephone booth and called her anyway. Perhaps it was fortunate for both of us that she was with a patient and couldn't possibly come to the telephone.

Perhaps. But I didn't want to bet her life on it.

If I just hadn't seen that bottle of Prince Ivan vodka . . .

I still had Jane Stevenson's house keys in my brief-case. But we'd released the house; that meant our consent-to-search no longer applied. I called Charles's Chips and asked where Zack Stevenson would likely have reached on his rounds, and then I went looking for him.

I found him, or that is, a Charles's Chip truck that I guessed must be him, parked behind a credit union. I waited, in my car behind the truck, for him to come out, and then I cornered him with another consent-to-search form. No, he hadn't lived in that house for a long time, but all the same he was the legal owner of it—by now we had checked on that—and he was still legally married to Jane Stevenson.

Looking puzzled, he said, "I already signed one of these. You already searched the house."

"Yes, sir, but now there's something else we need to look for." Yesterday, when we searched Jane Steven-son's house, I had never met Bradley Graves. If I had

seen a picture of Bradley Graves, I wouldn't have noticed it. And I certainly wasn't looking for one. Now
I am.

"Well, yes'm, you're welcome to look again. You
need me to sign this?"

"Yes, sir." I signed as a witness myself, which
meant the consent would not hold up in court if he
decided to challenge it, but he wasn't going to, and if
anybody else challenged it he'd say, in that same be-
wildered tone he was using now, "Yes, that's my sig-
nature."

If I remembered correctly, there were a lot of pictures in the house. I went looking for them. And
through them.

The only studio portrait in the house was an old
wedding picture, a slim (well, fairly slim) Jane
Stevenson and a much younger-looking Zack Stevenson. There were a lot of snapshots and school pictures, and I took the time to look through every one of
them individually.

I did find several pictures of Bradley Graves. But if
I confronted him with the pictures he could reply,
quite reasonably, yes, you already knew we were ac-
quainted. And I would have no answer, because the
indications were that Jane had been, surprisingly perhaps, a shutterbug. Besides Brad Graves, I also recognized Susan Braun and Olead Baker. In quite a

number of pictures a Trivial Pursuit game and a table of chips and soda pop were also visible.

She'd been taking pictures at Mensa meetings. There was no reason for Brad Graves *not* to be in those pictures.

And there was no vodka bottle, Prince Ivan or any other brand, full or empty.

SEVEN

I STARTED TO CALL Susan again. Obviously Susan wasn't going to listen to anything that might sound like an accusation of Brad, and she wasn't going to tell me anything about Corie Meeks for fear that would make her sound jealous of Corie. Which was ridiculous; any male who would pick Corie over Susan... But then once again I thought of Susan's general—and perennial—state of dishevelment, and wondered, What criteria? Whose criteria?

I didn't know what Corie Meeks looked like alive. I'd never seen her alive. Both Brad and Sam Barrett had assured me she had mental and emotional problems; though I wasn't sure I could believe Brad, I felt obscurely certain that Sam Barrett wouldn't lie to anybody for any reason.

So far, so good. But there were too many answers I didn't even approach having, too many questions I couldn't even formulate well enough to ask.

It was four o'clock in the afternoon. I ought to be going home. But could I, in all conscience, just go home, knowing that the killer—whoever the killer was—might strike again tonight?

I stopped at a 7-Eleven to find a pay phone. I called Matilda Greenwood first; she answered on the first ring.

"How many middle-aged or older women in your church live alone?" I asked without even identifying myself.

"Oh, dear," she replied, clearly recognizing my voice even without introduction. "Just about all of them."

"Just about all of them," I repeated, feeling rather pole-axed, though I'm not sure why, because everything she had told me should have led me to expect that very answer.

"Yes. And I know why you're asking because I've been thinking about that all day. Do you want me to warn them?"

"How many—"

"I told you, just about all of—"

"But *how many* is that?" I demanded, raising my voice more than I meant to.

"Oh. Oh, I see what you mean. About sixty. But I can reach all of them. Or most, anyway."

"You can reach sixty people between now and nightfall?" I asked, somewhat incredulously. This was, after all, late October. Daylight savings time was gone, and it was getting dark quite early.

"Oh, I don't have to call them all myself," she said, obviously surprised at the question. "I've set up a relay system. I have leaders I call—six of them—and each of them calls two people, and each of those people calls five or six. I can warn them all in about fifteen minutes. I've just got to make sure they realize it's critical they pass it on right now and not wait until tomorrow or the next day.''

Well. That was a surprise. That's the way my church—well, my son's church—does things, and it has given them the reputation of being about the most efficient raiser of volunteer labor in a hurry in the country. I was surprised though I guess I shouldn't have been, that Sister Eagle Feather's church had a similar system.

I called—or tried to call—Susan next.

She was busy with a patient and couldn't come to the phone.

That might be true. It might also be true that Susan, for any one of several possible reasons—but most likely the fact that she didn't want to look jealous of Corie Meeks—was avoiding me. I didn't want to think she was avoiding me because she suspected her fiancé; in fact, I didn't think that. If she really thought Brad was guilty, she would be helping me. So she didn't think that. But her not thinking it didn't necessarily prove it wasn't true.

I suspected her fiancé. And maybe it was just as well Susan didn't want to talk with me, because I was sure to let that fact out. Susan might be—probably would be—offended.

I didn't really want to offend Susan.

All the same, I had to locate, and warn, women living alone in that SIG group. Who did I know to call? Susan, who didn't seem to be speaking to me right now; Brad, who was the suspect; and Olead. It might be hard to get hold of a busy medical student. On the other hand, he sort of had to stay in touch because of his wife, who was expecting a baby soon. Very soon. Like next month.

I called their house, and Becky answered. "Hi, Mom," she said, cheerfully.

"Hi, daughter. How are you feeling?"

"Oh, just ducky-wucky. Jeffrey decided to draw a mural on the hall today."

On. Not in. I noted her linguistic precision.

Jeffrey, as I may have mentioned, is genetically Olead's half brother. Legally, he is Olead and Becky's son. Being adopted herself, Becky was rather pleased with the idea of having an adopted child. But being only nineteen herself, she does have her hands full. And Olead's millions of dollars don't help much with hiring servants if there aren't any available for hire, or if, as seems to be the case, both Olead and Becky feel uncomfortable with the idea of servants.

"What with?" I asked. Jeffrey's a little past the age at which the kids draw murals with the contents of their diapers, but one never knows.

"Crayons," she said. "I've been scrubbing for an hour and most of it is off. Do they make washable crayons?"

"How should I know? Hal's too old for crayons and Cameron's too young. They did for a while."

"Well, I'll go look for them when I have the energy."

"Is Olead around?" I asked hopefully.

"Uh-uh. He's not back in from school yet. Why? Did you need to talk to him?"

"Yeah, I need to ask him some questions. Becky, do you ever go with him to those Mensa SIG meetings?"

"I've gone a few times, why?"

I thought she had; I thought I had recognized the back of her head, leaning over the Trivial Pursuit board, in a couple of Jane's photographs. "Do you know how many women, oh, say, my age or older, who live alone, there are in the group?"

"I don't think there would be many," she said, "but I don't know for sure. Olead usually calls before he comes home, in case there's something I need. Do you want me to have him call you?"

"Yes, if you would," I said. "Or even, if he could come by. I'm on my way home."

"Okay, I'll—Jeffrey, put that down!" The telephone went dead.

Ah, the joys of motherhood.

I had succeeded in spending an entire day on the job without ever once setting foot in the police station. I had done it all in my car, with my own gasoline, and I was not going to get reimbursed. Although I did have to go straight to Corie's house this morning, theoretically I could, and should, have gone into the police station any time after that at least long enough to change cars and get my own hand radio, instead of this one, which, according to the white lettering on the side and bottom, had been issued to the uniform division. Someone there might well be wondering where it was by now.

Let 'em wonder. I'd turn it in tomorrow.

I would have to, anyway. These things have rechargeable battery packs, and each charge lasts, theoretically, about twenty-four hours. That meant that by tomorrow morning this radio wasn't going to be much use.

Come to think of it, I might need it during the night. I called Harry and asked him to tell Olead I was going to the station right now and would be home later.

In a less than hysterically happy voice, Harry said, "This is Thursday."

"Yes?" So it was Thursday. What did that mean?

"On Thursday," Harry said tightly, "I go to class."

"Oh, Harry! Oh my gosh! I didn't mean to forget—"

"I know you didn't, but how am I—"

"Isn't Hal there?"

"Hal has football practice. And before you ask, May Rector is grocery shopping. I checked on that already, too. And Lori is watching Hal practice football. Just a minute, I think I see May driving up." Silence, while he presumably went to the front door. "Okay, it is, 'bye."

Sometimes my life and Harry's life, and the combination of the two plus assorted offspring, get altogether too complicated. I needed to go home, but I had to go get a radio, and I'd have to figure out a way to get a radio without Captain Millner seeing me, because if he saw me he'd be certain to ask me about those reports I hadn't done yet.

I went to the police station. I put the uniform division radio back in the charger rack where it belonged, carefully changing its battery pack first so nobody would grab it thinking it was fully charged and find out the hard way it wasn't, and I got the little tape recorder out of my desk drawer and a couple of tapes so that if Cameron was asleep and Harry was at school and Hal was at football practice maybe I could get time to dictate some of the reports while I was at home.

I closed my desk drawer, stood up to leave, and practically ran into Ed Gough.

Of course, I jumped a foot. Wouldn't you? He's not that much bigger than I am, but he was altogether too close. And he'd come in completely silently, and besides that he was Ed Gough. If that means nothing to you, you are not female.

He stared at me with his usual reproachful expression. "I wouldn't hurt you," he said.

"I know that. You just startled me."

"You aren't wearing a green dress."

"How reassuring." He was still too close, and he smelled of Clorox. "What would you do if I was wearing a green dress?"

He didn't answer. He just looked at me.

"Ed, please go home," I said wearily. "I don't have time to mess with you today."

"She was wearing a green dress," he intoned. "Did you call that lady?"

"What lady?"

"That lady that was going to get me locked up."

Susan. I had been going to ask Susan about Ed Gough. "I've been trying to call her all day," I said. "She's been too busy to talk to me."

"Does she have a green dress?"

"I don't think she does, actually."

"Are you sure?"

"No, I'm not sure, but I don't think she does."

"Do you have a green dress?" He moved a couple of steps closer to me.

"Ed, I don't have a green dress and I don't want a green dress, now will you please go home and let me go home?" I shouted.

The noise attracted Ron Elgart from Intelligence. He stepped into the Major Case Squad room and said, "Ed, you're annoying the lady."

Ed turned to Elgart. "She doesn't have on a green dress."

"I hope you didn't want her to," Elgart said dryly. "Come on, Ed. I'll take you home."

"I can go home," Ed said, and shuffled out of the office, his clothes as usual a little too large for him, as if he had shrunk, and his gray hair sticking out in tufts from under his faded baseball cap.

"You okay, Deb?" Elgart asked.

I nodded. "Yes. But he's right, he does need to be locked up. He's getting crazier again."

"Ah, that's just Ed Gough being Ed Gough," Elgart said dismissingly. "He wouldn't hurt a fly."

"Yeah? Tell his sister that."

"Deb, that was . . ." Elgart had to stop and count. "Thirty-on years ago. He was locked up twenty-five years and never gave anybody any trouble, and he's been back on the street seven years and—"

"Gives people trouble constantly," I said.

"But that doesn't make him dangerous."

"Well," I said, "I'm not going to wear a green dress in front of him and find out."

Elgart laughed, and I took off down the elevator, headed for home.

Ed was waiting for me in the lobby.

It would be extremely silly for a policewoman—a veteran officer like me—to ask for an escort to her car. So I didn't. I merely sneaked out the back way and went around the building to my car, leaving Ed presumably standing in the lobby waiting for me.

On the way home, I told myself I was being paranoid. Why would Ed be waiting for me? More likely he was just standing in the lobby thinking what to do next.

But I still didn't want to wear a green dress to work the next day.

I was nearly home before I realized that what I should have asked Ron Elgart was whether he'd want his wife, in a green dress, to be in the same room with Ed Gough. The answer he gave to that might be interesting.

Olead's van was parked in front of the house when I got there. "Sorry," I said. "You can go on in, I just want to get the baby—"

"I've got the baby," he answered cheerfully. "When Harry wasn't here I figured I knew where everybody was."

Handing Cameron over to me, he unlocked the door with the key Harry and I had given him a long time ago. Over his shoulder, he added, "Is Harry mad at me?"

"No. He's just . . . He doesn't like the situation," I answered. "But . . ."

"I don't like it either," Olead said. "God knows I spent long enough with nothing left to me except my pride, and that was in shreds. I don't want to hurt his pride. But it's not his fault and—"

"Olead," I interrupted, "can we talk about something else?"

He stared at me. "I thought that was what you wanted to talk about."

"Then don't jump to conclusions," I said tartly.

He chuckled. "Okay. You got any Cokes? I'm dying of thirst."

"Let me check."

As I could have predicted, there were no Cokes. There was orange juice; catch Hal or Harry drinking orange juice if they can have Cokes instead.

Settled with a glass of orange juice, Olead eyed me intently. He'd changed a lot since I first met him; the self-confidence that was so fragile then hung on him now so heavily that it approached arrogance, but his blue eyes were just as direct, and his smile was far more free and open. "Is there a problem?" he inquired.

"What makes you think that?"

"You don't usually call before I'm even home and need to see me right then. Is it about Jane Stevenson?"

"And Corie Meeks," I said.

His smile faded. "Corie Meeks?" Then, explosively, he said, "Oh, shit!"

"That says something to you?"

He leaned forward and found a place on the coffee table, in and amongst Harry's assorted copies of *Soldier of Fortune* and *Brigade Quartermaster's Catalog,* to put the orange juice glass. "Deb, how much do you know about Mensa?"

"You ought to know how much I know about Mensa. Exactly as much as you've told me."

"Nobody else has told you anything?"

"Let's say if they have I'd rather hear it again from you. Fair enough?"

"Fair enough," he agreed. "Okay. Jane Stevenson was a pest. Corie Meeks is..." He eyed me. "Was?" I nodded. "Was," he said. "Was more of a pest. They were both insisting on forcing themselves into a group they didn't belong in and weren't happy in. But they weren't the only ones; there were others."

"Couldn't you... Wasn't there some way you could have eased them out?" I asked.

"That's what I'm getting to," he said. "If you'd join—"

"Olead . . ."

"Quit interrupting," he said without rancor. "I am about ninety-nine percent sure you're eligible. How do you spot people who are likely to be eligible for Mensa? Not by how they make their living. Not by what they do. Sure, Mensa is an organization for the superintelligent—that's a phrase that comes up a lot in discussions and in publications—but that doesn't mean it doesn't have a goodly sprinkling of nuts and flakes. Or have you forgotten I was simultaneously a member of Mensa and an inmate of a psychiatric institution?"

"I haven't forgotten," I said softly.

"Deb, the overwhelmingly omnipresent constant among Mensa members—and among Mensa eligibles who haven't joined—is *loneliness*."

"Loneliness?"

"Loneliness," he repeated firmly. "People are always using Mensa for a matrimonial agency. A few members gripe about it, but most see the necessity. As one woman who lived in a small town said to me one day, 'If I don't join Mensa I'll never meet a man I can talk with who isn't my brother.' If you're superintelligent, sure, you may well be happy with television and a six-pack, and baseball in the summer and football in the fall, just like everybody else, but you always want—you always *need*—something else, too. And

you may not even know what it is. All you know is
you're constantly, achingly, lonely."

"But I—"

"You're not lonely?" He sounded as if he couldn't
decide whether to laugh or cry. "Don't give me that.
Who's your closest friend?"

"Susan, but—"

"You were forty-one when you met Susan. Who
was your closest friend before that?"

I couldn't answer. Because the truth was I hadn't
had one.

"And that's my point, Deb. You're not quite as
much of a freak as I am—you've never been called
schizophrenic and locked up—but you're still a freak.
You never quite fit in anywhere. Everybody in the police department thinks you're weird because you make
these leaps in thinking nobody else makes. Sometimes they work out and sometimes they don't, but all
the same you make them and nobody else can figure
out where they come from. They think you're just
grabbing ideas out of the air. You can't make them
understand that there's a complicated process of reasoning behind those hunches you have, because nobody else can figure out the reasoning and you can't
explain it in ways that they can understand, so you just
sit there and let them yell at you about jumping to
conclusions. Right?"

I nodded, not trusting my voice to speak. I knew my eyes were full of tears, and I couldn't reach the Kleenex because my arms were full of baby.

"And that's what I'm telling you, Deb. That's what Mensa is for. I've heard people call it an elitist organization. Well, maybe it is elitist, but on the other hand, I know of very few organizations who'll take everybody who walks in off the street. Just about every organization is elitist in one way or another. Mensa happens to have based its criteria on intelligence—raw intelligence, as well as it can be measured. And by the way, whether you know it or not they've got nonverbal tests for people with learning disabilities, because an awful lot of learning-disabled people are still extremely intelligent. And what it is, is a refuge. It's a place to go where you won't be lonely. Where nobody is going to laugh at these wild leaps of thinking you make. Oh, they might disagree with you, they might argue with you till hell freezes over, but they're not going to laugh at you, because they make the same wild leaps themselves. So... Mensa is full of very, very, *very* lonely people."

"So you go to Mensa to feel ordinary," I heard myself saying.

He looked startled, then nodded. "That's about right. You go to Mensa to feel ordinary. If you can anywhere at all."

"What does that—"

"I'm getting there," Olead said. "What does that have to do with Jane Stevenson, with Corie Meeks? That's what you want to know? Just this: if you're that lonely, you're ... well, first you're kind of afraid to piss anybody off too much, because then they won't like you, and if you're that lonely you've got a real, real serious need for people to like you. But second, if you're that lonely, you realize ... comprehend ... grok ..."

I laughed out loud. He was quoting Heinlein's *Stranger in a Strange Land,* and I was surprised to hear it from somebody in his generation; that was a cult book when I was younger than he was now. *"Grok?"* I repeated.

"It means ... well ... comprehend and internalize. Sort of." He looked rather hurt.

"Olead, I know what it means," I assured him. "Okay. Go on."

"Okay, well, if you really comprehend being lonely, then you're more likely to have compassion for somebody else who's lonely."

"So you don't throw Jane Stevenson and Corie Meeks out of a group of mental health professionals even though you know they don't belong there."

He nodded. "Corie ... You've probably been told she was chasing Brad Graves. It was really embarrassing to watch. We all knew Brad had less than no interest in her; he's been in love with Susan for ... gosh, as long as I've been going to these meetings, and probably a lot longer than that. It's been Susan hesitating, not him, and not because she doesn't care about him, but because she just didn't seem sure she wanted to get married. Meanwhile Corie was throwing herself at him. It was pretty awful to see. And technically, she *was* in the mental health profession, you know. On the fringes—she was a secretary—but still she could legitimately say she was involved with mental health.''

"So even though she was embarrassing everybody and seriously annoying Brad Graves, nobody would try to ease her out of the group."

"Oh, we tried to ease her out," Olead said. "But according to the Mensa constitution there was no way to throw her out, even if any of us would have had the heart to do it, and it would have taken a cannon to successfully ease her out."

"A broken neck was equally effective," I pointed out.

Olead was silent for a moment. Then he said, "Yeah. For her and Jane both."

"Tell me about Jane."

He shrugged. "I told you about Jane."

"Tell me some more."

"What do you want to know? You saw her. It wasn't just that she was fat; lots of fat people look great otherwise. They dress well, take care of their clothes, take care of their hair, that kind of thing. I think she worked at looking as bad as she possibly could. And she smelled. Like she didn't bathe very often. I know she kept her house spotless. It wasn't just clean, it was nasty-clean, if you know what I mean.'' I nodded, and he went on. ''But I don't think she kept herself very clean. She was a terribly unhappy woman. I don't...I mean, look, I'm trying not to sound judgmental. But you need to know what it was really like. She...I know she was sick. She was emotionally sick as well as physically sick, and we all wanted to be extra nice to her because of it. That may have been a mistake. I don't know.''

''Olead, you've lost me completely. I don't even know what you're talking about.''

''We met at her house,'' he said carefully, ''because she wanted us to. Not very often, but often enough...too often, really. Nobody really minded her making people go outside to smoke; lots of people do it. For that matter I do; I don't like smoke and I don't want it around my family. But...I don't know why she wanted us to meet there. She seemed to think she was being hospitable, but she was driving everybody crazy. You didn't dare drop a potato chip crumb on her floor. You had to keep your soda pop can in your hand because if you set it down on the furniture it would leave a ring, and the idea of providing coasters wouldn't cross her mind. We couldn't play games on the table because it might get scratched, so if we wanted to play games we had to do it on the floor. But she wanted us over there. And she went to this spiritualist church. Deb, I don't know anything about survival after death. I mean, I've read about it, these near-death experiences and that kind of thing, and I'm not one of those people that thinks when you die you're gone like a blown-out match with nothing but the matchstick left to put in the ground. But it seems to me, when a person dies, that person's dead, just like if I moved to China I'd be in China and I wouldn't keep popping over to Fort Worth because Uncle... because somebody wanted to talk to me."

"So you think..." This really didn't have much if anything to do with my investigation, but it was interesting in other ways. And it might tie in, at that. Again, I was on a fishing expedition.

"I think death is moving away," he said precisely. "I don't see why if somebody's moved away they'd want to keep coming back. And besides that, if I was dead and somebody with a towel wrapped around her head and a burned-out thousand-watt light bulb on a table in front of her wanted to call me, why should I answer? It's always the tiresome ones who run to the mediums. The ones you probably didn't even want to associate with when you were alive, so why should you want to anymore when you're dead?"

I couldn't help laughing at that, and Olead grinned and shrugged. "Whatever. But you see what I mean. She'd gotten herself mixed up with this phony medium—"

"Whom I've met, and I'll bet you'd like her if you met her."

Olead made a face and then shrugged again. "Maybe. But anyhow, Jane had decided she was a medium herself. Both a trance medium and a channel medium. Also she had declared herself a faith healer, on what grounds I haven't the faintest idea. And by the way, I suspect faith healing very often works, not just on psychosomatic ailments but on some others too, because I don't think anybody really knows yet exactly how the mind and the body are wired together. So I'm not putting down all faith healing. Maybe I'm not even putting down all mediums. For all I know there might be some real ones, except in that case I don't think they'd have much control over what happens. But my point..." He hesitated. "I think what I'm trying to say is that whether or not there are real mediums, real faith healers, I don't think Jane Stevenson was one. And she was driving everybody nuts."

"Were she and Corie friends?"

"Well, some. They both went to that same spiritualist church. I think it was Corie who took Jane to the group to start with."

"How did Corie get in to start with?"

"Oh, Corie was in it before I was. Let's face it, legitimately she was involved in mental health care. Peripherally, but still involved." He looked at his glass.

"It's empty," I said unnecessarily.

"I don't exactly remember drinking it."

"Well, I certainly didn't. Anyway, I saw you do it. Do you want some more?"

"I guess."

"Do you or don't you?" I asked rather impatiently.

"Yeah," he said, and handed me the glass.

"Who do you think killed them?" I asked from the kitchen.

"I don't know. Are you sure the same person killed both of them?"

"We're never sure," I said, returning to him with the glass of orange juice. "But I'm reasonably sure, as sure as I can be without finding out who did it. Assuming the same person killed both of them, who do you think did it?"

"Deb, I'm not being coy. I honestly haven't the slightest idea. I can't really imagine anybody in our group doing it."

I sat down again, still holding Cameron. "Two women dead," I said. "Dead in identical, very unusual ways. Three connections between them. They belonged to this spiritualistic church. They both belonged to this Mensa SIG. And they both had more or less pissed off Bradley Graves.''

Olead drank some orange juice fast.

I decided to abandon Bradley Graves for the moment and return to him later. "If somebody else in the SIG group were going to be murdered," I asked, "who would you expect to be next?"

He shook his head. "No idea."

"And you don't want to think about it."

"You got that in one."

"Is there any other woman who is annoying people in anything like the same way?"

He shook his head.

"Other women, my age or older, who live alone?"

He shook his head again. "Susan theoretically lives alone, but of course she doesn't really. She lives at the clinic, and there's always people around there. I can't think of anybody else."

"Does everybody like Susan?"

"There's nobody everybody likes, including me and thee."

"In your opinion, would Bradley Graves kill?"

"Given the right—or perhaps I should say the wrong—circumstances, anybody would kill. Again, including me and..." he went silent. "Sorry, Deb. I wasn't trying to bring up bad memories."

I shrugged. "It happened. It's over. Thirteen months over, just about."

"Yeah. Right. You ought to get some counseling."

"I do not need—"

"Right, right, right." He held one hand, playfully, as if to fend off my defensive attack. "You do not need counseling and you never have nightmares and the moon is made of green cheese and I'm going out right now and slice some off to put on my pizza."

"Knock it off, Olead. I'm talking about Bradley Graves. Under what circumstances do you think he would—"

"Deb, I'm telling you, you're on the wrong trail. Brad did not kill either of those women."

"If he thought Corie was going to break up his romance with Susan—"

"He didn't think that."

"How do you know?"

Olead shook his head. "There are just things you know. And besides that, don't you think it would be stupid, if it was Brad, to kill two women known to be associated with him? And anyway, he wasn't any more aggravated at Corie than the rest of us."

"Olead, let me give you a scenario. Suppose there really was a little bit of fire to that smoke. Suppose Brad had, say, spent the night with Corie. Just once. If—"

"If Susan wasn't available?" Olead interrupted. "I don't believe it."

I could feel myself blushing. I certainly do not want to go around prying into my friends' love lives.

"All right, never mind that," I said. "Suppose, just for the sake of argument, that Corie had something on Brad. *Anything* on Brad. It might hurt him with Susan. It might hurt him professionally. Anything at all."

"Okay," Olead said, putting down the glass. His gaze on me was so steady I was uncomfortable.

"And the only way he could shut her up was to kill her. This is hypothetical," I added hastily, hearing Olead's indrawn breath as he started to answer.

"Okay," he said again, and let the breath out slowly.

"So if she was killed and nobody else was, then sooner or later the police would figure out that he was the one with the motive."

"Maybe."

"So he'd realize that. So what would he do? What would a smart man—let's say, a superintelligent man—do in that situation? Let it go, and let her blow the whistle? Kill her and hope to bluff it out? Or kill her along with two or three other women he didn't have any motive to kill, so it would all be put off as the work of a mass killer? A nut? Which would be the Mensa way to do it? Or are you going to tell me people in Mensa don't kill people?"

"I don't know of anybody in Mensa who's ever murdered anybody," Olead said, noticeably and carefully distinguishing—as I would have to myself—between *kill* and *murder*. "That certainly doesn't mean it wouldn't ever happen. I assure you there are Mensans in prison; some people even join there. And yes, maybe that would be an intelligent man's way of committing murder and hoping to get away with it. But Deb, that doesn't mean it's what happened, and I'm telling you, this time you're barking up the wrong tree. I've got to get home now." He got up, ambled into the kitchen, and put the empty glass on the counter. "I'll talk with you later, when you've had some time to think it over. But quit thinking about Brad Graves, because I'm telling you, the man didn't do it."

"I thought you said Mensa members don't laugh at other people's theories," I challenged.

"Mensans," he said absently. "I'm not laughing. I'm arguing. And I damn sure didn't tell you we don't do that."

As he headed for the door, I called after him, "Olead, are you trying to tell me that a psychiatrist who is a member of Mensa wouldn't ever, under any circumstances, flip out?"

He turned to look at me, his eyes suddenly unreadable. "No, I'm not telling you that," he said. "I can't even tell you for sure *I* won't ever flip out again. God knows I've done it before. But you know what? Objectively, I think I'm more likely to flip out than Brad Graves is. And suppose I did flip out and kill somebody, the newspapers wouldn't say 'Mensa Member Slays Whoever.' They'd say 'Former Mental Patient...'"

He was opening the door as he spoke, and I stood up, hastily. "Olead, I didn't mean..."

He smiled at me, but this time his smile was tired. "I know you didn't, Deb. And I didn't do it. This time or the other time. And neither did Brad Graves."

EIGHT

HARRY WOULD NOT BE HOME until nearly eleven o'clock. Hal... Let's see, football practice, he'd be home by seven, and he'd be ravenous. But it was only five-thirty now; that left me a little time to myself, as even Cameron didn't seem to be hungry. I'd decided to park him in his little sit-up chair so I could take him from room to room and let him watch what I was doing while I explained it all to him. I'm never sure how much he understands, but he coos and babbles enough to produce a semblance of conversation. When he got tired of sitting still I'd return him to the playpen.

I'm really not sure I like playpens, but with all Harry's electronic gear—ham radios, CB radios, soldering irons, tester circuits for this, that, and the other—it would be totally unsafe, for the baby as well as for the equipment, to turn him loose. I wasn't sure what we were going to do when he started walking.

The living room was superficially clean, which 90 percent or more of the time is all I worry about anyway. There were no dead newspapers lying around; most of Harry's *Soldier of Fortune*s and various survivalist and paramilitary catalogs were stacked more or less neatly on a shelf under the radio table. Even the dirty dishes had been not only returned to the kitchen but stuck in the dishwasher as well. The laundry, on the other hand...

As I think I have said, Harry does not do laundry. This is not a matter of male chauvinism. It is a matter of the peace of mind of all concerned, mainly me.

So I checked the laundry hampers, of which there are two, one in each bathroom. The one in the bathroom now used almost exclusively by Hal was nearly empty. I opened his bedroom door and hastily closed it again. I had found his dirty laundry.

Tough. It was going to stay dirty. As I have said before, I do not search bedrooms without a warrant.

On the other hand, I had to make him do something about the dishes in there, which were needed in the kitchen. Hmm. I'd have to ponder this matter.

With the first load in the washer, I sat down by the telephone. Had I, or had I not, done all I could reasonably do to protect the next potential victim of...whoever the killer was? I never had really thought it was Brad Graves; I had suspected him as a possible, not as a probable, and Olead had shaken me even on that. Matilda Greenwood still had not agreed to provide me the records of her ''church,'' and I still had not decided whether it would be worthwhile to apply for a search warrant.

Olead had told me he didn't think there were any women living alone who belonged to the SIG, other

than the two already dead. But his opinion was not
carved in stone. He is too young to pay attention to
older women, too married to pay much attention to
single women.

Somewhere there is bound to be someone who could
provide that information.

Did I dare call Susan again?

I could. I did.

Susan did not seem exactly cordial, until I told her
that since two women members of the SIG, both living alone, had been murdered, I wanted to see how
many other women living alone were in the group and
warn them to be careful.

Susan said she thought she could help me with that,
if I'd hold the line a couple of minutes. She did not
mention Brad Graves. She did not mention Corie
Meeks. I carefully didn't mention them either.

I waited, telephone to my ear, while Susan dug out
pieces of paper. It wouldn't take long; her office, unlike her person, is kept meticulously neat. Finally she
came back to the telephone and said, "You got something to write with? I want to give you an address and
telephone number."

The address was in Brooklyn. So, presumably, was
the telephone number.

"Is that an office?" I asked.

"Well, yes. You call the membership secretary, and they'll mail you a list of names and addresses, that is if they have—"

"Susan," I interrupted, "if that's an office phone number I can't call it until tomorrow. If they mail me a list tomorrow I'll be lucky to get it before Tuesday or Wednesday. Now what am I going to do in the meantime? Count corpses? Collect cadavers?"

"Oh," she said. "Oh, yes, I didn't think of that. Well, let me think . . . Deb, let me explain something about SIGs, okay?"

"Okay," I said resignedly. I was learning far more about Mensa than I ever wanted to know. Though come to think of it, just about every murder investigation causes me to learn far more about something than I ever wanted to know.

"The way a SIG works is, somebody decides it would be nice to have a SIG on such-and-such a topic. And then that person registers it with Brooklyn. And that person—the same one that thought up the idea— usually continues to run the SIG until he or she gets tired of it or until somebody else decides to take over."

"A dictatorship?" I asked.

"Oh, no," Susan said. "More like controlled anarchy. Anyway, that person keeps the membership list and sends copies of it to Brooklyn periodically."

"Okay, so who—"

"That's the problem," Susan said. "Ezra Loundes founded the group."

"And he's dead." I remembered talking with Samuel Barrett.

"And he's dead. I suppose somebody got the list after he died, but I don't know who."

"Look, if nobody was in charge, how did you all decide—"

"Controlled anarchy," Susan interrupted. "I can't tell you who was and wasn't on the rolls, because SIGs theoretically operate by mail, nationwide. It may well be that nothing on paper's been updated since Ezra died, and that's been over two years. But I can tell you the names of the people who usually came to the meetings."

I had no doubt that she could. Susan's memory is fantastic, and presumably I did not need the nationwide rolls. "But do you know who does and doesn't live alone, and what their telephone numbers and so forth are?"

"No," Susan said, "but—"

"Then what good is that going to do?"

"You'll see," Susan said smugly. "Can you come over?"

Not very easily, I thought, and explained.

"Then I'll come see you," Susan said. "There in forty-five minutes." She hung up before I had time to warn her that arriving in forty-five minutes would put her into competition with a very hungry and very large teenager.

Oh, well. I had time to provide for said teenager. I checked the refrigerator to make sure (a) that I still had hamburger meat, and (b) that it was still edible (yes on both counts), and then I made four large hamburger patties, put them in the broiler pan, and stuck them in the oven. They'd be ready about the time Hal came charging in the door starving. Four quarter-pound hamburgers ought to hold him until I had the time and/or energy to start thinking about supper.

You think I'm kidding? Obviously you have never been the mother of a six-foot-five (he's held that height for six months now, so he might really be through growing), sixteen-year-old football player. A *husky* six-foot-five, sixteen-year-old football player.

Then I grabbed a piece of paper and a pen. In my most formal memo style, I wrote:

TO: Hal
FROM: Mom
SUBJECT: Room
(1) Your room is pigpenocious.
(2) If I find it necessary to produce a warrant to
    search your room for dirty clothes, all clothes
    found on the floor will be jailed.

(3) They will be released only on payment of a suitable fine (of work). Otherwise they will be impounded for a period of one (1) week.

(4) In the meantime you may have some difficulty finding anything to wear to school.

That should produce the desired results. Hal, like most boys his age, is vain—I have seen him admiring himself in the bathroom mirror while hunting a whisker or two to shave off (in that respect, and very few others, his Oriental genes seem to dominate). The threat of impounding his school clothes would be far more impressive than the threat of grounding him, if only because he knew I really would do it. After due warning, that's what I'd done in May. And in view of the fact that Harry and I are attempting to impress upon him the importance of keeping one's commitments, we really can't ground him very effectively.

I taped the note to his bedroom door. Then I went and turned on the fire under the teakettle so that I could make herb tea when Susan arrived. I got out the Red Zinger, put a teabag in each cup, and waited.

Hal arrived first. He dashed straight toward his bedroom, paused, and (predictably) howled. "Oh, Mo-o-om!" He managed to get about six syllables, each full of measurable anguish, out of "Mom."

Of course, I didn't respond. He changed clothes, and I could hear the sounds of stupendous bangings and thuddings from both his bedroom and the bathroom, combined with occasional profanity I pretended not to hear, before he emerged some five minutes later to take a bulging trash bag—complete with the note I had just written—out to the garage where we keep trash until pickup day. He made two trips to the kitchen to pile dishes on the counter; then, catching my eye, he put them in the dishwasher, added soap, and turned the dishwasher on. He then stalked back to his bedroom for another thirty seconds before returning to inform me that his room was clean.

It wasn't, of course, but it was enough better to be acceptable. He'd arrived home a little earlier than I expected; I should have time to get the laundry sorted and out to the garage, where the washing machine lives, before Susan arrived. I took three laundry baskets—for white, light-colored, and dark clothes (Hal would produce a full load of each)—into the bathroom, as Hal headed for the kitchen to attack the hamburgers. I did find occasion to ask if he intended to wash the sneaker I found among his clothes, and if so where was its mate, but other than that the job seemed to be reasonably complete.

Susan, on the other hand, was a little later than I expected. I had just finished moving the first load to the dryer and putting the second load in the washer when she drove up. Hal rushed to open the front door for her, and she let Pat in. The dog, of course, darted

to the playpen to sit down beside it and adore Cameron, who offered his hand to be licked. When I started
to remove him (the dog, not Cameron), Cameron
started to howl.

I know when I am defeated. I let Pat stay.

Harry would be furious at that. He would call it a
breach of discipline, which it undoubtedly was. He
would assure me that if we would always keep the dog
out, then the dog would learn he was not allowed in
and would stop trying to come in.

I don't believe that for a minute. We have followed
that policy for two years, and Pat still tries to run in
every time the door is open.

Susan sat down and produced, from her capacious
purse, an 8½1/2-by-11-inch paperbound book with a
sheet of paper clipped to it. The paper looked like a
computer printout; it had all those infinitesimal knobs
where the tractor-feed sheet is torn off, and where the
sheet is separated from the one above and below it.
Noticing the direction of my gaze, Susan said, "I don't
have the list on computer. I just used the computer
while I was working with it, so I could keep them in
alphabetical order."

She handed me the list. Women. Names only. No
addresses, no telephone numbers, nothing to indicate
whether they lived alone. My face must have shown
my dismay, because Susan said, "That's only half the
job. Here's the other half."

With the paper-clipped sheet removed, the book's title, *Mensa Register,* was now visible. She opened it and pointed to a name at random. Following it was a line of letters and numbers. "Coded information," she explained. "Here's the breakdown of the code."

About that time, Pat, nails clicking on the vinyl flooring we'd put down when we all got heartily sick of the old ratty brown carpet, temporarily abandoned Cameron to go over to beg some hamburger from Hal. Hal, who was not about to share his hamburger with Pat, put the dog out, and of course Cameron howled and I had to pick him up.

It took a couple of hours and several telephone calls before we were sure that we had located, identified, and warned all the women in the SIG who were living alone. We called every woman whose information indicated she was single, widowed, or divorced; most were living with parents, children, or roommates, and the three who were not agreed to leave within an hour and stay with friends for at least a week, or until the newspapers indicated the killer had left off or had been caught.

By that time I had changed Cameron two or three times, fed him, and put him down for a brief snooze. Hal, having (he said) done his homework at school, had taken off to go walking with Lori.

"Now what about the men?" I asked.

"I didn't do the men. You didn't ask for them. What do you need the men for?"

Was Susan being deliberately obtuse? "Somebody killed those two women," I said. "The only point of contact between them—the only points of contact, I mean—are the SIG and the spiritualist church. Therefore the killer has to be in one or the other, and I've got to get a complete membership list of both."

"That's not correct, you know," Susan said.

"What's not correct?"

"That those were the only points of contact. You know Corie introduced Jane to the group."

"And they met at church."

"How many other people—how many other women—go to that church?" Susan asked me.

"I don't know, sixty-odd I think, but—"

"Proximity isn't enough," Susan said patiently. "There had to be something else, something to make them feel they were, or could be, friends. Otherwise why would Corie have bothered?"

"Maybe she didn't. Maybe they were just talking one day and Corie happened to mention the SIG and Jane asked—"

"Why were they talking? Look, you didn't know Corie Meeks. I did. She was strange—"

"So I've been told," I interrupted.

"But besides that, she was selfish," Susan said. This didn't sound like jealousy, not coming from Susan,

and I listened intently. "She never did anything unless she got something out of it. She wouldn't have
talked with Jane unless she got some advantage out of
talking with Jane. She certainly wouldn't have introduced Jane to the SIG unless she had a good reason
for doing so."

"Maybe the advantage was that she looked a lot
better compared to Jane than she would look if she
were the only outsider in the group," I suggested.

"Oh, she wasn't the only outsider," Susan said.
"See, the thing is, a SIG has to be open to anybody—"

"Anybody?" I interrupted.

"Anybody in Mensa," Susan corrected. "Any
Mensan who is interested. It couldn't be just for mental health professionals; in order to be chartered it had
to be for people *interested* in mental health care.
Which means it not only got health care provid-
ers..."

"It also got health care consumers?" I asked, when
she hesitated.

"Exactly," she said. "So we had a few that seemed,
well, odd even to me, and I've seen just about everything. We have this one guy who asked me one time to
help him commit himself permanently, and of course
I couldn't do that except under very tight court super-
vision. He committed himself to a state hospital for six

weeks and then came right back to Mensa. Just fo
example.''

Well, that takes care of Ed Gough's question,
thought. He couldn't be locked up permanently an
more than that person could.

"So back to Corie, what I'm saying," she went or
"is that there had to be some underlying similarities
and the relationship, or whatever it was, had to be o
benefit to Corie, or it wouldn't exist at all. And if the
had underlying similarities, and if a relationship ex
isted, then almost certainly there were other points o
contact than the two you know about."

"Those are still the only two I have to go on, Su
san," I said. "Can you produce a list of men..."

I stopped. She was shaking her head. "I don't knov
everybody," she said. "First time I can break awa
long enough tomorrow, I'll call Brooklyn myself an
get a list over the telephone. But I can't produce on
out of my head. I'm sorry, Deb. I just can't."

I invited her to stay for supper, and she decline
very politely. "Are you mad at me for suspectin,
Brad?" I asked.

She looked startled. "I didn't know you suspecte
anything like that. That's silly, Deb. He wouldn't—'

"Olead agrees," I said. "But I've got to go o
looking."

Susan shook her head. "It's a waste of your time.
guess I would be mad if it weren't so silly. But that'

not why I'm leaving. I've got a meeting next month, and I'm writing a talk for it. I have to work on it. Really."

I thanked her for coming over and for the help she'd provided, and watched her leave.

What else could I do?

WHAT ELSE, INDEED? I wondered, when the telephone rang at one-fifteen in the morning.

IN THE CAR, using the small radio I'd brought home in the afternoon, I could hear Bob Castle from ident arriving at the scene, asking whether the ME was en route yet, being assured that he was. Other than that, Fort Worth seemed to be pretty quiet.

I stopped long enough in the front yard to get the patrolman stationed there to give me a briefing—a more-than-usually thorough one from a patrolman, because he'd been the first officer on the scene.

He said Captain Millner had decided not to come out, had decided Detective Ralston could handle it.

How nice of him to say so, I thought sarcastically, and went on inside.

After a brief glance at the victim, Mary Beth Toomer, forty-two, who was lying on her back in a tightly made bed in a spotlessly clean house, I turned my attention to her adult daughter, Eileen, who was sitting on a couch in the living room with her hands clasped tightly and resting on the dark green wool of her slacks. "I'm Deb Ralston," I told her, parking myself beside her. "I'm the detective who'll be working on the case. I know this is a terrible time for you, but do you think you could possibly manage to answer a few questions?"

Her dark eyes focused on me slowly, and then she nodded. "Yeah," she said. "Yes, I can answer some questions."

"You're Eileen Toomer?"

She nodded.

"Do you normally live here, or—"

She shook her head. "I go to Texas Woman's University," she said.

"In Denton?"

"The school's... The main school's in Denton. But I'm in the nursing program, and we have several campuses. I'm at the one in Dallas."

"Parkland, is that right?"

She nodded again.

"And that's where you normally live, the TWU dormitory at Parkland?"

"Yes."

"But you decided to come home tonight?"

"Yes." She rubbed her hands together and then rubbed them on her knees again. "I didn't have anything I needed to do on campus tomorrow. And I had a date tonight. My boyfriend lives in Fort Worth, he goes to T-Com..."

She paused, apparently not sure I knew that T-Com as the Texas College of Osteopathic Medicine. "Yes, my son-in-law goes there," I told her. "Go on. You ad a late date, and so your boyfriend brought you ome instead of..." I stopped. She was shaking her ead.

"My boyfriend hasn't got a car," she explained. "I ave the car. So I... After I got through at the hospital today, I came back to Fort Worth, and I came by he house, but Mom..." She paused, choking back ears. "Mom wasn't home, so I just changed clothes nd went to pick up Bob, and then we went to a movie nd then we, we just, we just went and sat in the car, nd, and talked, you know, and then I came home bout eleven-thirty and I thought Mom was asleep. I ought she was asleep."

Eileen sobbed a couple of moments. I got up and oked for a box of Kleenex, found it, and brought it ack to her. Then she said, "She's got this medicine he has to take at midnight. She doesn't usually forget it. I mean... I mean she didn't usually forget it. he's... She had epilepsy real bad, and if she didn't ke her medicine exactly every six hours, well, you now, it was bad. And she didn't get up at midnight take it. Usually she doesn't even need the alarm, but e always sets—set—it. Most of the time she'd wake p before it went off, and get up and take the medine and then turn the alarm off so it wouldn't ring.

She keeps—kept—it . . . the medicine, I mean, but th
clock, too, for that matter . . . in the kitchen, so sh
couldn't go right back to sleep and forget it, and if sh
doesn't—didn't—wake up without the alarm, then th
alarm would wake her up and then she'd get up. B
she didn't get up. I didn't think anything about it
first. I just thought my watch was five or ten minut
off, but . . . it wasn't supposed to be.''

No. Nurse's watches are supposed to be extreme
accurate.

''So I waited. She didn't get up. And the alar
didn't go off. Then I thought, well, it was after eleve
thirty before I got in, maybe she took it early, just b
fore she went to bed, but . . .''

''She didn't do that?'' I asked softly, when Eile
paused.

''No. She . . . she didn't do that. She took it at no
and midnight, and six A.M. and six P.M. on the dot
mean, she'd even, like, leave a meeting or chur
service long enough to take her medicine on time. S
said that was the least disruptive schedule she cou
think of, and she said if she did it that way every tir
then she wouldn't risk breaking the habit. So when s
didn't get up, I kept waiting. I . . . Finally I went in t
bedroom to check on her, and . . . she wasn't breat
ing. She . . . I would have done CPR, but . . . it was t
late. I could tell. It was too late. So I . . . I went a

called nine-one-one. I didn't know what else to do... I didn't know what else to do.''

She was sobbing again. Tears were falling unheeded onto the nice green cable-knit sweater, carefully selected to complement her dark red hair and brown eyes, and onto the nice green-and-yellow plaid pants that matched the sweater so well. I got her another Kleenex, and she took it mechanically, wiped her eyes, blew her nose.

Then she looked up. "Why are all the police here?" she asked. "Do you usually do this much just when somebody dies?"

"Not this much, no."

"Then why..."

I didn't want to tell her. I did not want to tell this girl, not much older than my younger daughter, that her mother had almost certainly been murdered.

Of course, I told her anyway. She stared at me in total disbelief, and then asked, very quietly, "Why?"

I had to tell her we didn't know why. Probably if we knew why, we'd know who, and we'd be able to stop it.

This is not my favorite part of police work.

I waited for her sobbing to let up again, and then I asked, "Is there somebody you'd like us to call for you? A relative? Somebody from your church? Your boyfriend?"

"Not at this time of night," she said. "I'll call them tomorrow. There's no use doing it right now. What could they do?"

"Let me ask you just a couple of questions, and then I'll let you get some rest."

"Ask all you want to. I don't think I'll . . . I don't think I want any rest right now."

"What church did your mother go to?" I asked.

"First Presbyterian. We've always gone there."

"She couldn't have changed lately? You would have known?"

"Of course I would have known. She's . . . She was a Sunday school teacher."

"Was she a member of Mensa?"

"What's that? Anyway, she wasn't. She didn't belong to any clubs except the women's group at church, and that volunteer thing she did."

"What volunteer thing was that?"

"She was a volunteer receptionist at this mental health clinic. I don't know much about it. I don't even know if it was charity or if it was county or something like that, because she just started it after Dad . . . died . . ."

Her voice started quavering again. Mechanically I put yet another Kleenex into her hand. My mind was working at a hundred miles an hour. Volunteer receptionist at a mental health clinic.

Susan had been right. There was another connection.

Rank hath its privileges. It was Dr. Davisson, not Dr. Habib, who came in with a new medical examiner's investigator following on his heels.

They didn't need me for this. And I couldn't start asking the appropriate questions, of the appropriate people, until morning, unless I asked more questions of Eileen Toomer, who didn't look to me like she was up to answering questions.

I don't know what *you'd* have done with Eileen Toomer. *I* certainly couldn't go off, leaving her alone in the house where her mother had just been murdered. What I finally did was, I took her home with me and put her to bed in what had been my daughters' room before they had married and moved out.

I then went back to bed, figuring I'd lie awake until morning thinking. But the next thing I heard was Cameron trying out his voice preparatory to howling for breakfast.

NINE

IT WAS ONLY SIX O'CLOCK; I didn't need to leave for another hour and fifteen minutes, and I still had at least half an hour of blessed silence before Hal came banging back in from his early-morning religion class. Last year they were studying church history; this year they seemed to be on the Old Testament. Hal had enjoyed Genesis and Exodus, which were gory enough even for his somewhat morbid teenage imagination, but he was bored out of his mind with Leviticus and wasn't spending nearly as much time as usual telling me things I did not want to know.

I couldn't help wondering what was going to happen when he got into all those prophets. One of my neighbors had told me that when her son, now in college, was that age, he gobbled up, believing every word of them, all those silly paperbacks that purport to prove that Ezekiel and probably all the other prophets were running around in flying saucers. I'm not sure Hal would get ahold of the paperbacks, though I'm sure he would believe them if he did happen to read them.

Of course, I was wondering all this while I was feeding Cameron. A hungry baby has no interest whatever in delay of any kind.

I don't usually make much of a breakfast on weekday mornings. Harry, now at home all day, has gotten to where he likes to eat later; Hal prefers peanut butter sandwiches for breakfast, and I'm perfectly happy with a bowl of Cheerios. But I don't usually have in my house a young woman who has arrived home in the middle of the night to find her mother dead. Should I feed her or not? I wasn't sure what Miss Manners would advise in a situation like this.

Well, I could make a big breakfast and try to pretend I did it every morning (except that Hal would certainly sabotage that pretence), and then if she didn't want it she could always have Cheerios. Yawning— Cameron had lately begun snatching the bottle from me and insisting on holding it himself, so I put him down and let him do it—I opened the refrigerator and got out a pound of bacon. Unlike milk, bacon is perfectly safe from unauthorized teenage depredations. Catch Hal eating anything he has to cook himself— unless, of course, he is on a camping trip, which makes the situation totally different.

I have quit making biscuits with buttermilk. Yogurt works just as well, and it seems to keep a lot better. Besides that, if I don't happen to be making any biscuits, I can eat it with fruit instead. I am told that some people drink buttermilk, straight from the carton. I'm not sure I believe that.

I got out the baking powder and soda and stopped to think again. Having come of age in the sixties, I am, despite my job and my loathing for the drug culture, in many ways a child of my generation. This means that I am a little distrustful of white flour. It looks sort of nasty to me. I always make pound cakes so I can use whole wheat flour, and of course I always make whole wheat biscuits.

Maybe I should make white flour biscuits for Eileen Toomer, who wasn't even born in the sixties.

I got out the cannister of white flour I keep for those few occasions I absolutely have to use it. Maybe it would have weevils—which I usually refer to as weasels, due to some linguistic confusion that erupted when my older daughter was learning to talk—so that I would be relieved of having to make the decision.

The white flour did not have weasels or weevils. But it looked altogether its usual nasty self. I couldn't face it at this hour of the morning. I shoved it back on the shelf, got out my usual whole wheat flour, and began to make biscuits, trying not to think about the case I was working on. Sufficient to the day—or the hour—is the evil thereof.

Eileen Toomer wandered into the kitchen, wearing, of course, the same green slacks and sweater she had worn last night, because there was nothing else for her to wear unless she wanted to run about in her under-wear, something modest women usually do not wish to do in a strange house. "Could I help you with that?" she asked, very properly.

"Thank you, but this is a one-person kitchen," I told her. "It was really difficult when my daughters were still living here, because two people don't fit in here."

The kitchen, in fact, is horrible. It is long, at least in comparison to its width, and narrow. One end is open to the alleged dining room, which in turn is open on one side to the living room, and the other end consists of the doorway to the garage, which tells you exactly how wide it is not. The sink and counter are on one side, with the alleged pantry, about the size of a coat closet, between the counter beside the sink and the door into the garage. The wall opposite the sink contains a cooktop, a built-in oven, and a refrigerator in a nice little niche so that you can't put it anywhere else. The refrigerator also is right beside the door to the garage. This means that the pantry door, the refrigerator door, and the garage door all open into the same space. On top of that, from the front of the oven to the front of the sink opposite is exactly wide enough to open the oven door, which means you have to stand sideways to the oven to put anything in it. You can imagine how much fun that was when I was pregnant.

Need I add that Harry selected this house as a surprise to me and then picked me up at work to tell me he had bought it?

And to this good day he can't figure out why I hate, loathe, despise, and abominate the kitchen.

There's not even enough room to remodel it, because that side of the house sits approximately three feet from the property line.

Enough about my house and my kitchen. It should be quite evident that I was in a crummy mood and did not want to think about the case. Only an immense desire to avoid thinking about the case would have me now stuffing biscuits into the preheated oven, standing side on to the oven, as usual, at this ungodly hour on a Friday morning.

Biscuits in. Fifteen minutes. Bacon in the microwave. If I didn't use the microwave for anything else, I'd own one just to cook bacon in. I used to always burn the bacon because it is so sneaky, going from stubbornly raw to charcoal in seconds.

Cameron began to complain. Holding his own bottle was losing its charm. Tough, kid, you shouldn't have volunteered. Eggs. Ugh. Eggs look nasty in the morning, at least before they are cooked.

How many eggs? Harry (who is large, but who should be watching his cholesterol). Eileen Toomer. Hal, who is an army in himself. Me. And I don't really like eggs.

What the heck. I got out eight, broke them into a bowl and dropped the shells down the disposal. Somebody else could turn the disposal on later. The noise is too much for me early in the morning.

Scrambled. I was definitely not up to anything else. I think I'm allergic to morning.

Cameron was no longer fussing. I glanced into the kitchen to see that Eileen had picked him up and was talking to him. That was probably good for her. Babies are usually good for whatever ails women, as long as it's not contagious.

The front door banged; Hal was returning. Someday, maybe when he's forty or so, he will learn how to shut a door without making it sound as if he shot it.

Stall. Stall. Stall. I did not want to go back to the house I'd last seen about two-fifteen this morning, which come to think of it was only about four hours ago. No wonder I was so sleepy. I did not want to take Eileen into that house.

All the same, I ran out of ways to stall, and we were pulling up into the driveway by a quarter to eight. A patrol officer was still guarding the front entrance; I had no idea whether the rear entrance also was guarded or whether it was just locked. The ident car was sitting beside the patrol car, so apparently Bob gave up on it last night, as frequently happens when the light is too bad; and somebody from day watch, most likely Irene, was on it.

It was Irene. "What rooms are you through with?" I asked.

"Everything but the bedroom," she answered. "I've been out here since six. Deb, it's a wash—"

She stopped, looking at Eileen. I introduced her, explained.

"What's a wash?" Eileen asked.

"I was going to say washout," Irene answered. "I don't know what Deb's told you, but we're not getting fingerprints. Somebody comes through and scrubs everything. That seems to have happened here."

Eileen nodded. "I should have noticed that last night," she said, her voice reasonably steady. "Mom...Mom's really not a very good housekeeper, and the house seemed lots cleaner when I got back in than it did when I left in the afternoon. But sometimes she gets—got—in these sprees when she cleaned like mad, and if I noticed at all, I just thought she must have done that. Is it...is it okay if I...if I do something? So I don't have to just sit here?"

"Of course," I said. "That's what I was asking about. Anywhere except her bedroom. You can't go in there."

"I'll have to later," Eileen said, "to get something for...for the funeral."

"Later's fine," I said, feeling horribly awkward. "Just not now."

Eileen drifted out of the front room, and I stood and watched Irene for a minute, unsure whether to see if there was something else I should do around the house or whether I should go start knocking on doors. Really, I ought to wait about another half hour before doing that, because people getting ready to leave for work would not be willing to talk with me, and people getting other people off to school or work would be more likely to be talkative after the other people had departed.

Eileen came back into the front room. "Deb," she said, "there's something funny."

"What is it?" I asked. "Something funny" at a crime scene is almost always important.

"In the bathroom," she said. "I thought I would, you know, do the laundry, and... Look." I had followed her into the bathroom, where she had begun to sort laundry in the bathtub. "I thought... I thought it would make sense to do the laundry. There's no sense just letting it sit. And then I noticed." She gestured at the bathtub.

"Noticed what?" I asked.

"Mom always does—did—her laundry on Saturday," Eileen said. "Today's Friday. She always wore a dress or a skirt and blouse to work. She took a bath every night and then put on fresh clothes the next day. She would never wear the same clothes twice in a row. Except nightgowns; she'd usually wear the same nightgown all week. She doesn't have anything that has to go to the dry cleaner. She wears slacks on Saturday. So this hamper should contain everything she's worn, except nightclothes, since last Saturday. It should have slacks for Saturday, a dressy dress for Sunday, and a dress or a skirt and blouse for each day from Monday through Thursday—four days. And it should contain six sets of underclothes, Saturday through Thursday. The six sets of underclothes are here. Here's the slacks and blouse. Here's the dressy dress. I was home Sunday; I know that was what she wore to church. But there's only three other dresses here. One of her dresses, or skirt and blouse sets, is gone. I...I thought it might be important,'' she finished, looking anxiously at me.

"It's very important,'' I answered hoping my tones didn't sound as grim as the thoughts in my head. Stepping back out of the bathroom, I called to Irene. "Did you fingerprint the laundry hamper?''

"What on earth would I do that for?'' Irene asked. "No. I didn't.''

"Then come do it right now.''

I should have known what we'd get. I guess I did know, in one part of my mind, but I hoped to be wrong. I wasn't wrong. Scrub marks. Nothing but scrub marks, except the clear, fresh prints of a young nursing student who'd opened the hamper moments before. He—whoever he was—had scrubbed everything he even might have touched.

But when did he do it? That was the problem now. Eileen got home about eleven-thirty; he was gone by then. "What time did your mother normally get home on Thursday?" I asked.

"It varied. The clinic stays open late, but she doesn't stay that late. She hates driving during the five o'clock rush, and since she's working on a volunteer basis they can't very well demand she stay later. I left the house about three-thirty, and she wasn't home then. So...call it four, maybe as late as four-thirty if she stopped at the grocery store on the way home."

"Which grocery store would that be?" Maybe I was looking at the wrong set of connections. Maybe Mensa, Sister Eagle Feather, mental health, were all a bunch of coincidences. Maybe the real link was something else entirely, something I had no way of knowing—the same doctor, the same dentist, the same grocery store clerk, the same UPS delivery man.

"Usually the Winn-Dixie just a couple of blocks from here."

She gave me the address, and I nodded. "Do you know what the dress would have looked like?"

"I couldn't possibly know that," Eileen answered, "I haven't lived at home for the last three and a half years. She's probably changed two-thirds of her wardrobe. Some of the new clothes I've seen, some I haven't. So I could look in her closet for the next week and couldn't begin to guess what might be missing.''

That sounded final.

All right, what to do now? I had to go talk with neighbors. But in this working-class neighborhood, that might be better done after six, or maybe even sometime Saturday, when I wasn't scheduled to work but certainly could come in anyway. For now...

We knew—or at least were almost certain—that Jane Stevenson's last set of daytime clothing, whatever it might happen to be, was missing. But I hadn't checked to see if there was anything missing that ought to be in Corie Meeks's apartment, and I was sure nobody else had checked either.

''Who are you going to call to stay with you?'' I asked Eileen.

''What?''

''You said you would call somebody—''

''Oh,'' she said, ''yes, I did. Just a few minutes ago. I called my aunt. But she lives in Tyler, and she said it would be this afternoon before she could get here.''

Irene probably would be through with her work in another hour. And I didn't, for some reason I couldn't clearly define in my own mind, want Eileen Toomer left alone in this house. Oh, of course, eventually she would have to be left alone. But not quite yet.

''I need to get a written statement from you,'' I told her, not entirely mendaciously, ''and I need to check on a couple of other things on the way to the police department. Would you mind too much if I took you with me and let you wait in the car while I—"

"Just let me get this in the washer first—"

"I'd rather you wouldn't wash anything yet."

"If... If he did take something, I can understand why you'd want to know what it was, but what difference does it make what he *didn't* take?"

"Take my word for it, it does." In the first place, the only chance we'd have of demonstrating to a jury that he *did* take something would be by careful enumeration of what he *didn't* take, coupled with Eileen's precise knowledge of her mother's habits. And besides that, there was that old theory of fiber transfer. What else might he have touched, while he was taking what he took? What might he had left...

I didn't want to explain all this. I just asked Eileen to come with me. I was halfway to Corie Meeks's apartment before it dawned on me Eileen might have wanted to change clothes herself.

Never mind. She could change clothes later.

Things I wanted to check: (1) Was there any evidence that any clothes were missing from Corie Meeks's apartment? (2) Was there any evidence to suggest what grocery store or stores she shopped at?

Come to think of it, there was one more thing I had better check. Had we released the apartment yet? If so,

I would have to get a new search warrant before I could go back in.

I radioed in. Dispatch checked with my office and assured me that although we no longer had an officer at the scene, we had not yet formally released the apartment. That meant the door had yellow evidence tape over it, which would not keep a fly out if the fly wanted in, but would serve to warn law-abiding citizens that their presence was not desired.

I stopped by the apartment office and asked the manager, Sue Jarvis, for the key to Corie's apartment. She looked doubtful. "You still have Corie's key," she pointed out.

"I don't know whether we do or not," I said, which was quite true, as I had not been involved in whatever inventory of her property had taken place. "But if we do it's there and I'm here. I really have to get in there again, and all it'll do is waste time if I have to go to the police station and get whatever key we have there."

She still looked doubtful. I reminded her of the evidence tape, of the fact that she could not clean and rerent the apartment until we were through. She looked aghast at the thought of rerenting it, which interested me. But finally she gave me the key. "Remember to give it back when you're through," she said.

"I'll do that," I promised. "But you do intend to change the locks, don't you?"

"Change the locks?"

"In case the killer has Corie's key."

I thought for a minute she was going to faint. But she recovered. "Yes," she said, "yes, we're going to change the locks, of course. But really, I don't know whether we're going to want to rent the place again, anyway. I mean, people are..."

"Funny," I agreed. "Yes, they are. To be honest, I wouldn't want to live in it myself."

Leaving Eileen Toomer in the car in the visitors' parking spot, I walked on over to Corie Meeks's apartment, unlocking the front door and leaving it open as I stepped inside. It was dark inside, and already, in a day, it had developed that musty odor that afflicts vacant, locked-up buildings. There was really no reason this place should smell of corpse, because there had been no bleeding and little if any discharge of body fluids. At the most, the body had lain there less than twelve hours. But to me the smell was there. Faint, but definitely there.

I turned on the living room light, not because I was superstitious—I am not—but merely because it was dark in there.

The bathroom, where the hamper presumably was, was located off the bedroom. I didn't bother to turn on the bedroom light. I could see well enough to get to the bathroom, and once there, of course, I turned on the light over the sink.

The hamper, pink plastic imitation wicker, sat against one wall. I opened it and gingerly began to lift out one piece at a time, sorting it into separate piles in the bathtub exactly as Eileen Toomer had done.

A pair of pink bikini panties. A beige bra. A pair of blue bikini panties. A—

Abruptly, the light in the bedroom went on.

And off. And on again, precisely as Sue Jarvis told me the lights had done the night Corie Meeks died.

Feeling my heart pounding, the hot perspiration of an adrenaline rush pouring over me, I flattened myself against the bathroom wall and drew my pistol.

The light went off. And on, this time to the accompaniment of a strange wailing moan. My heart rate felt like it was now up to about five hundred beats per second.

I couldn't do a dramatic Dirty Harry act, slamming the bathroom door flat against the bedroom wall, because the door opened into the bathroom, where I was. So the best I could do was jerk the door open, fast, with my left hand, while I held my little Smith and Wesson two-inch K-frame in my right hand, and yell, "Freeze!"

A very large Siamese cat—male, unneutered—stopped wreathing itself around the lamp long enough to look at me with startled but still insolent sapphire blue eyes, yowl, and resume wreathing itself around the lamp, which turned off, and on, and off, and on.

My gasp turned into laughter, and the sweat turned cool. "You silly animal," I said, "what in the world are you doing?" I approached, and the cat growled.

"Now you stop that." I touched the lamp. It went off. I touched it again. It went on. The cat growled at me and resumed playing with the lamp itself.

One of those touch lamps. I'd seen them advertised. You don't have to fumble for the switch at night; all you have to do is touch it anywhere and it comes on. I had told Harry, the first time I saw them advertised, that anybody with a cat would be crazy to get one, because the cat, as soon as it accidentally figured out how the lamp worked, would play with it from then on.

It appeared that I was right.

And that we could change our estimate not of when Corie died but of when her killer left. As long as the light was burning steadily, the killer was there. Only after the killer left did the cat go in and play with the lights, trying to wake Corie up.

Was that why this door had been left unlocked and open, unlike the doors to the other two places? Because of the cat? So the cat could get in and get to its food dish, which the killer had apparently refilled, and its litter box, which the killer had evidently changed?

A very solicitous killer. He kills the woman, then he cleans the house and tends to the pets.

I went back to the bathroom and resumed sorting laundry. In all, I found five pairs of panties, three bras, two pairs of slacks, one blouse and one dress.

Apparently Corie Meeks was rather erratic in her clothing habits. There was no way whatever I could tell whether anything was missing, not unless I could find out what she was wearing on the last day of her life and see if it was present.

Her phone was still connected. I telephoned Samuel Barrett. He answered the phone himself; apparently his nurse or receptionist or whatever was out. I asked my question.

"Why do you need to know that?"

"Because I do. Take my word for it."

"Sorry," he growled. "I haven't the slightest idea."

"You didn't ask her to wear white?"

"Have you ever seen Corie Meeks in white?"

"Obviously I have not."

"Take it from me, she'd scare my patients. No. I did not ask her to wear white. But as to what she was wearing, I'm sorry, but I honestly don't know. Camille—that's Camille Ventris, my other secretary—she might know, but she's not here."

So much for that. I thanked him, hung up, and spent a few minutes—well, actually it was probably a few seconds—thinking. That friend of Corie's who lived in another apartment... What was her name? Genny, Genny Cantrell. Maybe she would remember.

And maybe she would know what we should do about Corie's cat.

She didn't remember what Corie had been wearing. Ten to one she hadn't seen Corie in two weeks. And the cat? She drew back. "Not that cat," she said. "Nobody wants that cat. It's mean."

Well, maybe. Siamese cats usually aren't, but every now and then one becomes very, very possessive and acts strange about things. "What's it's name?" I asked.

"Satan. Now, that should tell you something."

All it told me was that Corie Meeks had an odd taste in names for cats. I could not see myself sitting in Corie's bedroom calling, "Satan..."

Satin. I would call it Satin. That's close enough not to confuse the cat unduly, and I felt a lot happier about it.

I returned to Corie's apartment. I had shut the door behind me when I left to make sure the cat stayed in. I probably needn't have bothered. The cat was in the kitchen, crouched over its bowl, industriously crunching. "Hello, Satin," I said.

The cat glanced at me, growled, twitched its tail slightly, and went on crunching.

I looked in Corie's cupboards, found a can of tuna, and looked in a drawer for a can opener. "I'm a friend, Satin," I said. "See what I've got?"

I have never met a cat that wouldn't abandon absolutely anything, with the possible exception of a cat of the opposite sex at the appropriate time, for tuna. Satin was no exception. He leaped lightly onto the counter, which apparently was where he ate tuna, and yowled. I set the open can down in front of him, and he went to work on it, growling deep in his throat as he ate.

I left him to it and checked briefly for grocery bags. There were none. Returning to the telephone, I called the water department to see if anybody could remember what Jane Stevenson was wearing the last time she was there. Nobody could remember. It probably didn't matter anyway; she was probably killed on Saturday, and nobody from the water department would have seen her on Saturday.

Recalling my husband's favorite imitation profanity when he is watching his language in front of children, I said, "Rats, bats, and Democrats," and went back to the cat.

Who growled at me.

"You ungrateful feline," I said, and went looking for a cat carrier, finding it in a hall closet. It took me another couple of minutes to figure out how to work the door. That involved a lever and a spring strong enough that even the most enterprising cat, able to figure out that the people pushed the lever in order to open the cage, would not be able to push the lever itself.

Never mind how long it took to get the cat into the cage. Suffice it to say that both the cat and I were out of breath, I had several scratches, and small bits of fur were floating in the air by the time we got through. And I'm glad we can't understand what cats are saying. I was sure this cat was using dreadful language.

I still wasn't altogether sure what I would do with him. If he were a normal, nice, friendly Siamese cat I would give him to one of my daughters, but I didn't want a cat that acted like this around my grandchildren.

I remembered a Siamese tomcat we had when Vicky was little. The cat was run over when it was about two and a half, and Vicky and I both were inconsolable. I didn't really want another cat after that, because it seemed disloyal to the cat we'd had. Anyhow, one time I'd seen—from too great a distance for me to object successfully—Vicky hauling that cat down the stairs by its tail. The cat had its ears laid back, but that was its only protest. When Vicky turned it loose, the cat got up, strode a few feet away, and sat down to lick its rumpled fur back into sleekness.

The cat followed Vicky everywhere; it went to bed with her at night, woke her up in the morning, sat down on the floor beside her and purred as she watched TV. It was an altogether trustworthy, gentlemanly cat.

Satin wasn't.

Come to think of it, I had no right to decide what became of Satin. Corie Meeks's heirs and assigns, whoever they might happen to be, had that responsibility. I would just put Satin in a boarding kennel. At least he'd get fed while somebody decided what to do with him.

But I'd do that later. For now, I'd go on to the police station, taking Satin with me, to get that statement from Eileen that I hadn't really needed until she noticed clothing missing, and then get her back to the house to stay with her aunt.

I took the carrier to the car. Eileen, waiting patiently, said, "Hello, kitty." Satin growled at her and went on swearing.

I put the carrier in the backseat. Feline profanity rose around us, especially when I started the car.

Most likely the only use the carrier had had was to take Satin to the veterinarian, where he was subjected to various indignities including shots. Cats do not approve of shots. Cats do not approve of any indignities.

This cat's person was dead. This cat's living arrangements had been upset. This was not a happy cat.

And he made sure we knew it.

As I was in my personal car, I could not park in the enclosed, shaded police garage, which in turn meant I could not leave Satin in the car. Even in October, a closed car becomes an oven, a lethal chamber for pets and children, very quickly. So I had to take him in with me.

We—Satin, Eileen, and I—went in the front door of the police station, and with a sinking feeling I noticed the grotesque figure of Ed Gough, looking more and more like that glum fellow in *L'il Abner* who always used to have a small rain cloud directly over his head. I hoped Ed wasn't waiting for me. Maybe I could sneak by him unseen.

Ha.

Ed spotted me and headed straight toward me. Then he stopped, looking at the carrier. ''That's a cat,'' he told me.

''No shit, Sherlock.'' Satin was continuing to yowl.

Ed looked hurt. ''You said a bad word.''

''Ed, would you please, please, pretty please, go home?''

''Hello, cat.'' He tried to stick a finger into the carrier.

Satin, of course, growled and cowered into the back corner of the cage. Well, that was a slight improvement; at least he hadn't bitten Ed's finger. Though come to think of it, he didn't bite me either. Scratch, yes, bite, no. "Ed," I said, "the cat is very unhappy."

"Cats don't like cages. You should let him out of the cage."

"I have to find a safe place to do that first. But you let the cat alone."

His face sad, he backed away from the cage. Then he noticed Eileen. His mouth opened, hung open as if he had forgotten how to close it. "Green," he said. He took a step toward her.

I handed the cage to Eileen. "Get on the elevator," I told her. "Push the button for the fourth floor. I'll call up in a minute."

She didn't understand the urgency in my voice, but she took the cage and headed for the elevator. "Green," Ed said again. He started to follow her. The look on his face frightened me.

"Ed," I said, "you go home right now. You go straight home. I'll come talk to you later this afternoon about what we can do to get you locked up."

Because I was sure now that he was a clear and present danger, and I was sure I could convince whomever I had to convince.

But why in the world did I have to cope with that right now, on top of everything else?

It wasn't until I got in the elevator that I began to worry. What if Jane Stevenson, Corie Meeks, and Mary Beth Toomer had all been wearing green?

Oh, that was absurd. The one person we knew he had killed was a girl. He noticed girls. These were all middle-aged women, late-middle-aged women, older than I am. He couldn't...

Could he?

Could he?

TEN

I DIDN'T HAVE TO TAKE Eileen home. She called home to see if her aunt had arrived; her aunt had, and came to get her. They were going to a funeral home to make arrangements.

I was glad I didn't have to go.

I sat at my desk and assembled notes before beginning to dictate my reports. But I didn't get very far, and after a while Dutch Van Flagg asked me what was wrong.

I shrugged.

"Don't give me that," Dutch said. "You don't sit at your desk and mope unless something's wrong."

Still I hesitated. Then, abruptly, I said, "What if it's Ed Gough?"

Dutch stared at me for a moment, and then began to laugh. "Deb, you don't really believe that, do you? Because if you do, you're crazier'n he is."

I wasn't laughing. "I don't exactly believe it, Dutch," I said. "It's just... I don't have any other suspects. He's killed before. And he tried to confess to these, only I wouldn't listen."

"Right," Dutch said. "And why wouldn't you listen? Because he's confessed to about nine hundred other murders that he didn't do. He's confessed to strangling women who had been shot. He's confessed to murdering women who weren't even dead. You know that as well as I do."

"I know that," I agreed wearily. "But what's to stop him from—"

"Deb, how in the world could he have done it? He didn't even know any of these victims."

"I don't know that and neither do you. We don't know who he does or doesn't know. Anyway, they could be random. He didn't have to know—"

"So random he just happened to pick three women who lived alone, and at least two of them and probably all three—"

"Mary Beth Toomer didn't—"

"Mary Beth Toomer lived alone," Dutch interrupted. "It was pure luck her daughter picked this weekend to come home. And just because she wasn't in Mensa doesn't mean she didn't know the other two. There's bound to be another connection."

"There might be. That doesn't mean there's bound to be. And the clothes—"

"Aren't green dresses. All three women were in nightgowns."

"Which might have been put on them after death. And at least two of the women had clothes missing, apparently the last clothes they'd worn during the day."

"I didn't know that," Dutch said.

"So now you do. I couldn't tell you for sure about the other, but I think she did too."

"Were they wearing green dresses?" Dutch challenged.

"I don't know yet. But what if they were, and he saw them and followed them home?"

"You don't know what they were wearing," Dutch said. "And even if they were wearing green dresses, how many women in the city of Fort Worth are wearing green dresses on any given day?"

"But I saw him when he saw Eileen Toomer. And she wasn't even wearing a dress. She was just wearing green."

"Deb, you're reaching. That's just plain silly. There's no reason in the world to suspect Ed Gough."

"I don't know about that." I picked up the phone, dialed Samuel Barrett's office from memory, and got a hardware store. I looked up Barrett's number and tried again. This time a woman answered. What was her name, Barret's other secretary? Camille. Camille what?

Camille Ventris. "Are you Camille Ventris?" I asked.

"Why do you want to know?"

Cautious, this lady. "I'm Deb Ralston, Fort Worth Police Department," I said. "I'm working on—"

"Oh, yes, Corie," she said, not sounding particularly grief-stricken. "How can I help you?"

"Can you remember what she was wearing..." I had to stop and think back. Thursday? Was it Thursday morning we'd found her body? It had to be. Monday Jane's body was found, but it wasn't until Wednesday we knew it was murder, then Thursday morning Corie, then Friday morning just after midnight Mary Beth...

A sudden thought chilled me. A murder on the weekend, probably Saturday. A murder Wednesday night, a murder Thursday night... Were there two or three more bodies we hadn't found yet? Or had he for some inexplicable reason waited until after the first murder was publicized before going on with the others?

That didn't make sense.

"What she was wearing when?" Camille asked me. "You mean Wednesday? The last day she was at work? I'm not real sure... It might have been that green dress, but I can't say for sure. I just wasn't paying any attention."

"Did she have several green dresses," I asked, "or just one?"

"Of course, I can't say for sure," Camille said, "but the best I can remember there was only one. It was really ugly, a green cotton paisley print with maroon splotches on it. I can't imagine why she liked it

so much, unless it reminded her of her youth o
something.''

A green cotton paisley print with maroon splotche
on it. There certainly hadn't been one in the laundr
hamper, but she might have hung it back in the close
or even pitched it down in the bedroom, which
hadn't checked that thoroughly. Of course, the crim
scene crew would have seen it, but seeing and notic
ing aren't the same thing. Not if they had no reason t
know it was important.

Go back to her place and look? I would have to
Camille wasn't sure she had worn the green dres
Wednesday, but I could be sure whether or not it wa
in the apartment. And if it wasn't...

This time I didn't want to go through Sue Jarvis t
get the keys. Let's see...I already knew Eileen didn
have any way of determining what her mother wore o
Thursday, and I'd get to the people where she worke
later. Bev might know—not what Jane had bee
wearing on that Saturday or Sunday, we already kne
she didn't know that, but at least whether Jane had
green dress, and possibly Bev would be able to...

I got Corie's key out of property. I didn't have to g
Jane's key because it wouldn't do me any good if Be
wasn't there with me, and Bev had a key to Jane
house.

But there was no use calling Bev until I had first verified whether Corie's green dress was missing.

"Deb," Dutch called after me as I went out the door, "are you seriously trying to pin it on Ed Gough?"

"Not unless he did it," I replied. "But if he did, then I sure want him off the street." Then, remembering the way he had looked at Eileen, I corrected myself. "I want him off the street anyway."

"So what are you going to do?"

I told him.

"You going to go see Ed Gough?"

"I hadn't planned to."

"Well, let me go with you. If Corie's green dress is nice and safe in her apartment—and I'll bet five dollars it is—then there's no sense worrying him. But if it isn't, well, I'll just take a little trip with you to look at Mr. Ed Gough."

"Let me call Bev first," I said, "and let her know I'll be calling her later, so she won't head for home without . . ."

Dutch shrugged and watched me call Bev. I didn't get her alarmed. I just told her I wanted to call her later after I'd checked on something, and asked her not to get out of reach. On impulse, I picked up a Polaroid somebody had taken of Ed Gough several months ago and stuck it into the notebook in my purse. Then I picked up the keys to the detective car I was supposed to be using, and Dutch followed me out the door and down to the parking garage. I left the cat behind, asleep.

I didn't want to think about what the rest of the Major Case Squad was going to stay to me if the cat woke up and resumed swearing in my absence.

The yellow tape was still on the apartment door, where I had secured it again after entering earlier. The dirty clothes were still in the bathtub where I had left them. And since we hadn't released the apartment yet, we were still operating on the original search warrant. I actually wasn't sure who had taken it, but I could find that out later and add to its receipt anything I removed from the apartment.

Dutch knew what we were looking for. He began crawling around looking under furniture and in dresser drawers, while I methodically began to check everything in the closet.

Thirty minutes later, both Dutch and I were prepared to swear there was no green paisley dress—and no other green dress of any description—in Corie Meeks's apartment.

And that was interesting.

"You want to go talk with Ed now?" Dutch asked me.

"You owe me five dollars."

"I'll go on owing it. You want to go talk with Ed now?"

"Not yet." Using Corie's telephone, I called Bev again. This was a number I really did know by heart.

She answered on the second ring, very properly. "Medical Examiner's Office, may I help you?"

"Bev? Deb."

"What—"

"We're still thinking about the missing clothing," I interrupted. "Do you know whether Jane had a green dress?"

A long silence, before she repeated. "A green dress?"

"Yes. Don't ask me why right now."

"All right. Yes, she did."

"Just one, or more than one?"

"Just one that I know of. I liked it on her; it was one of the few things she had that didn't make her look fatter."

"Can you describe it?"

"I guess. Dark green, woven jersey rather than knit, long sleeves, jewel neckline, gathered skirt. That's about all I can say."

"Would you recognize it?"

"Of course, but why? Have you got it?"

"No. I want to see if it's still at the house anywhere. Can you meet me there?"

A long silence, then, "Deb, Jane's funeral is at five."

I looked at my watch. Almost three. No wonder she was hesitating. "Then I guess this would be a bad time—"

"No worse than any other," Bev interrupted. "I can leave work right now. I didn't have to come in at all, but I couldn't think of anything else I wanted to do. I can meet you there at the house in about twenty minutes. It's just that I can't stay long."

"It shouldn't take long," I said.

It didn't. By three-forty-five we were sure—all of us, Bev, Dutch, and me—that the dark green jersey dress was not in Jane Stevenson's house.

Ed Gough wasn't impossible anymore.

We weren't by any means ready to take a warrant, but he wasn't impossible anymore.

Bev headed for the funeral. Dutch and I drove to the run-down old house off Berry Street where Ed Gough had lived all his life.

No telling whether he would be there, or whether he would be back down at the police station trying to haunt me again.

Before we got out of the car, I asked Dutch. "Why did you come with me?"

"Just in case," he said cryptically. Then he added, "Deb. Ed Gough isn't very big, but he's bigger than you are. I wouldn't want you to become a statistic."

Some policewomen might object to that attitude as sexist. I didn't consider it sexist; I considered it practical.

Ed was at home. He came to the door, accompanied by two cats and a strong smell of Clorox, and stood there looking at Dutch and me. "You can't lock me up today," he said at once. "I have to feed the cats."

"Well, now, we weren't planning on locking you up right this minute," Dutch drawled. "So you've got plenty of time to feed the cats."

"Good. I have to scrub the floor, too."

"Can we come in?" I asked.

"Yeah. You can come in. I did it, you know. I killed her."

"Who?"

"That lady. But she wasn't wearing a dress. She was wearing green but it wasn't a dress. She was wearing pants." He looked at me disapprovingly. "Ladies aren't supposed to wear pants. Ladies are supposed to wear dresses."

"How did you kill her?" I asked. I'd explain later, to Dutch, about Eileen, whom Ed definitely hadn't killed.

"I didn't mean to. But she kept yelling and yelling and so I had to stop her from yelling. I didn't mean to. But I heard her neck break. It cracked like hail on the roof."

"Who else did you kill?" Dutch asked.

"That lady."

"Which lady?"

"A lady."

"Was she in bed?"

"Certainly not. Ladies don't go to bed when they have company."

"Can you show me where she lived?"

Ed looked confused and then shook his head. "Uh-uh. I forgot."

"Did you keep her dress?" I asked.

"I kept all their dresses."

Dutch glanced at me. "Will you show us their dresses?"

"You won't take them away?" Ed said. "'Cause I need them."

"What do you need them for?"

"I need them," Ed repeated. "So you can't have them. But I'll show them to you."

We followed, as he led us to a bedroom and threw the door open. "This is her room," he said proudly. "But she won't let me clean it. I can clean the rest of the house, but not her room." He stood aside to let us in. Involuntarily Dutch choked, and I'm not sure I didn't. From the smell, and the appearance, it literally had not been cleaned in nearly thirty years. It must have been his sister's room. Cosmetics, combs, and brushes from the fifties littered the dresser, and old yellowed magazines partially covered the sheets on the unmade bed, which had darkened with age.

Somebody, almost certainly Ed, had driven nails at regular and close intervals into the molding that fitted into the angle between the walls and the ceiling. Hanging from every nail was a green dress. The dress itself. Not one of them was on a hanger.

None of them was paisley. None of them was a solid, dark green jersey. And every one of them had a Goodwill price tag hanging from the sleeve.

I pointed to one of them. "Where did you get this one?" I asked.

"Off her," he said, "after I killed her."

"When was that?"

"I forget."

"What did she look like?"

"Pretty."

"How old was she?"

"I don't know."

"Was she my age?"

"Uh-uh."

"Older or younger?"

"Younger. And she didn't say bad words. You say bad words. I hear you saying bad words."

"I'm not saying bad words now," I pointed out.

"Sometimes you say bad words. It isn't pretty to say bad words. I only kill pretty ladies."

"I'll keep that in mind," I told him. "Thank you for showing us."

"I have to scrub the floor now."

As Dutch and I headed for the front door, I had a glimpse of Ed Gough on his knees in the kitchen, reaching in a bucket of what smelled, from this distance, like pure Clorox. He drew out a dripping brush and vigorously applied it to linoleum that was already almost faded white.

"Shut up," I told Dutch on the sidewalk.

Dutch wasn't laughing yet, but his face told me he was only waiting to be sure he was absolutely out of earshot of Ed Gough before he began to laugh. "Goodwill," he chuckled. "Goodwill. He buys 'em from Goodwill and makes up fairy stories."

"All the same, he killed his sister, and all the same, those two women are missing green dresses, and all the same, those green dresses are apparently what they were wearing just before—"

"But he only kills pretty ladies," Dutch interrupted, buckling his seat belt. "Would you say Jane Stevenson—"

"Dutch, would you please just shut up?" I turned left.

"Where the hell are you going? The station is *that* way."

"Goodwill isn't," I retorted.

"Just why do you want to go to Goodwill? Deb, you never give up, do you?"

"No," I replied. "I never give up. If you wanted me to, tough."

He didn't go into Goodwill with me, which was rather unfortunate, because I had an interesting visit there.

No one paid me any attention when I first walked in. There was no reason why anybody should notice me. I was just another shopper. But when I stopped the manager, an otherwise attractive woman who seemed to have a rather severe case of cerebral palsy, and got out my badge and the picture of Ed Gough, the reaction was interesting. She called, or beckoned, to three other women—one with the thick lips, strange eyes, and protruding tongue of the severely retarded, one who held a paralyzed left arm out at an alarming angle, and one who looked perfectly normal as far as I could see—and they all crowded around the picture.

"He comes in here pretty often," the manager told me, forcing the halting words out.

"He like green dress," the retarded woman said. "He always want green dress. I don' like him." She slapped at the photograph, nearly knocking it from my hand.

The other two women agreed, and then the retarded one spoke again. "I scared him."

You're scared of him? I thought, but wasn't completely sure, that that was what she meant.

Apparently it was; she nodded vigorously, and the one with the crippled arm said, "He scares everybody."

"What does he do that's scary?" I asked.

"He doe'n't *do* anything," the manager said, unable this time to force out the *s* sound, which turned into a glottal stop. "It't the way he look't at people."

"I know exactly what you mean," I said. "Have any of you ever been wearing a green dress when he came in?"

The retarded-looking one nodded vigorously.

"What did he do then?"

"Follow me. Inta the bafroom."

"I had to get him off her," the normal-looking one said suddenly. "I think he was trying to, you know, but thank goodness she doesn't understand..."

The retarded-looking woman immediately made it plain she did at least partially understand. She explained in slightly mispronounced gutter language, exactly what she thought he was trying to do, and she did not mince words. Ed would definitely consider that she was using bad words.

At any rate she was using very explicit words.

"He had his hand't up on her neck," the manager got out. "We all...*h*ad to...*h*elp pull him off." It was now *h*'s that were giving her trouble, besides *s*'s. I admired her persistence in speaking at all.

"Would you be able to swear to that in court?" I asked.

The manager stared at her in blank amazement. "A jury?" she got out. "You think a jury would—"

"Not a jury," I interrupted, perfectly aware of what she was thinking, that the average citizen confuses cerebral palsy with mental retardation and does not realize that behind that halting speech, that staggering walk, is a perfectly normal and often above-normal intelligence. "A judge. The man who comes in here is mentally ill, and from what you tell me, it's not safe for him to be on the street. But I need more people than me to testify to that."

"We'll testify," the normal-looking one said grimly. She nodded toward the retarded-looking one. "They might not believe *her*. But she does know what happened to her. And so do we."

I got names, addresses. Whether or not Ed Gough was the killer, whether or not I ever managed to catch this killer, at least I was going to get Ed Gough back off the street. Because I was certain now that if I didn't get him off the street, whether or not he killed recently, he was ready to kill again.

"You look like the cat that ate the canary," Dutch told me, as I turned the key in the ignition of the police car.

"I'm not. But I'm going to get Ed Gough off the street."

"That won't clear these cases."

"I'm still not sure of that."

"Bet you ten dollars."

"You never paid me the five dollars."

"I'll win it back."

"Pooh."

But that reminded me of Matilda Greenwood, and after we arrived back at the station I picked up the telephone and called her. "Is there anybody in your church named Ed Gough?" I asked.

"Not that I know of," she replied promptly. "But some of them come a time or two and never tell me their names, and some of them stick around for months before they want me to know who they are."

"He looks like Joe or Ed or whatever-his-name was Bliffistick, if that was his name. You know, in *Li'l Abner*."

"I haven't the slightest idea what you're talking about," she replied.

"The little guy with the last name composed entirely of consonants. Isn't he the one the cloud always follows?"

"I don't read comic strips."

It probably wouldn't matter if she did. The best I could recall, I had been in junior high, which placed it sometime in the late fifties, last time I had seen the little guy with the cloud. I gave a more precise description of Ed Gough.

"I would remember somebody that looked like that," she said.

"I expect you would, at that."

"So I never saw him before. Sorry. If I do see him, you want me to call you?"

"I guess." If she had never seen him before, it probably wouldn't matter.

I called Camille Ventris, who referred me to Samuel Barrett, who, not unexpectedly, told me he couldn't possibly release information on his patients. "Can't you even tell me whether or not *he* is your patient?" I demanded.

"Sorry."

"Can you tell me he is not your patient?"

"If I told you somebody was not my patient, the next time you asked me and I refused to tell you that person was not my patient, then you would conclude that person *was* my patient. I can't tell you anything about my patients."

"Even whether they killed somebody?"

"No."

"Even whether they were getting ready to kill somebody?"

Hesitation. Then, finally, he said, "If I had reason to believe one of my patients was going to kill somebody, and the killing was preventable, then I would let the police know, but I would also let my patient know I had let the police know.''

How positively ducky. He would let the patient know the police knew, so the patient could go out and find somebody else to kill. Integrity—I love it.

I tried to call Eileen Toomer. She wasn't home.

It was after five. I was supposed to be home. I was supposed to have left work over an hour ago. I called Harry and told him I was delayed and didn't know what time I was going to get home. He said, ''Surprise, surprise, surprise.''

''Oh, stop it, Harry, I'm not doing it on purpose.''

''Captain Millner told you to work late?''

''No, but if I come home somebody else might get murdered.''

''And if you don't come home you might get murdered. By me.''

''Stop it, Harry,'' I repeated crossly. ''I'll get there as soon as I can.''

''Call me before you leave the office.''

''I will. But it might be pretty late.''

''Ask me if I'm surprised.''

I said good-bye and hung up, feeling like crying. Why did he have to be nasty to me when I was doing the best I could?

I wanted to call the place Mary Beth Toomer worked, but it was too late—no it wasn't, or at least it might not be. Eileen had told me it stayed open late.

The trouble was, with everything else that was going on, I had failed to get its name. I called Eileen again; this time she was home.

It was called the William James Clinic, and it was set up, financed, and staffed by a group of psychiatrists in private practice who'd agreed to donate at least four hours a week to try to make psychiatric services more available to the poor. That didn't sound to me like anything the aristocratic William James would be terribly interested in, but perhaps I did him an injustice.

I looked up the number and dialed. A harassed but competent-sounding female voice, with chaos in the background, answered on the second ring. "William James Clinic, Joy Krupka speaking."

"Ms. Krupka, I'm Deb Ralston, Fort Worth Police Department."

"Can you hold, please." Without waiting for an answer, she turned away from the telephone; I could hear her shouting. "If you can't keep that child quiet, please take him out in the hall for a minute. Now." Her voice was louder. "What are you calling about?"

"Mary Beth Toomer."

"Oh, yes, that was terrible. She was such a good woman. There was just no reason for anybody to hurt her. Do you have any idea yet who did it?"

"We're working on some leads, but nothing's sure yet. Ms. Krupka, do you happen to—"

"It's Mrs. Krupka," she interrupted. "I think *Ms.* sounds really silly, don't you?"

"It's useful when you don't know much about the person you're talking to," I pointed out, "and lots of women like it. It doesn't really matter to me. I'm Mrs. Ralston at home and Detective Ralston on the job."

"Detective—oh, how nice. Now, you were saying..."

"That I need to know what Mrs. Toomer was wearing yesterday, if you can remember."

"Oh, yes, of course I can remember. It was brand new. She'd just gotten it at Dillards at the end of September, when the first fall sale started, and it looked so nice on her."

"What was it?"

"Oh," she said, "it was this gorgeous dark green wool. Solid green, and she wore it with an emerald silk paisley scarf and an emerald scarf pin. I mean, a *real* emerald. I wish I could afford to dress like that. But there, it didn't do her any good in the end, did it?"

"No, ma'am, it didn't," I said. "Does the William James Clinic have a patient named Ed Gough?"

A long silence. Then she said, "We're not allowed to release any information about our patients. You'd have to talk to the director."

"And who is that?"

"Well, Ezra Loundes started it, but after he died his partner, Sam Barrett, took over."

"Thank you," I said.

"Did you need anything else?"

"Not that you can give me. Thanks." I hung up and sat with my hand on the phone, thinking, before I called Susan.

She was much more cordial once I explained to her that her fiancé was no longer my suspect. She listened to me as I told her, without mentioning his name (if psychiatrists can be picky so can I) about Ed Gough's conduct in the police station lobby, about what the women at the Goodwill store had told me. "Yes," she said, "it sounds to me as if he certainly represents a clear and present danger. There shouldn't be any trouble getting a committal order."

"Do you think he's likely to kill again?"

"It sounds to me as if there's no doubt he is ready to kill again. From what you tell me, it was only those other three women who stopped him from killing that poor little girl in Goodwill."

The poor little girl was at least thirty. But Susan was right; mentally she was, and always would be, a child, a helpless child at that.

"He's been asking for years to be locked up," I said, "but we couldn't get anybody to do it. I even took him into court myself once, and the judge refused to sign the committal order. The trouble is, he kept confessing to every murder that happened, as well as a lot that didn't, and everybody thought he was just a harmless nut."

"Did you?"

"Sometimes. Other times . . . I wasn't sure."

"You should have talked to me."

"That was before I knew you."

"Oh," Susan said. "You know, if I didn't know better, I'd think you were describing Ed Gough."

I don't know what I said. I don't know if I said anything; I must have, because Susan said, "What?"

"Do you know Ed Gough?" I got out.

"Why, yes. He came to the Mensa meetings. He's this weird little guy with some kind of fetish for Clorox—"

"*Ed Gough* belongs to Mensa?" I interrupted.

"Deb, just about all of us—at least Olead and Brad and I—tried to tell you that intelligence and sanity aren't necessarily the same thing. Most intelligent people are also sane; despite some popular stereotypes, the percentage of mental disturbances among the superintelligent is acutally probably lower than among the less intelligent, but still—"

"Susan," I said, "I didn't ask for a lecture. I just want to be sure I'm understanding you correctly. Ed Gough not only is a member of Mensa, but he also was coming to your SIG meetings?"

"That's what I'm trying to tell you," she said. "Deb, are you saying you *were* talking about Ed Gough?"

"That," I said grimly, "is exactly what I am saying. All right. It's six o'clock now. Last night by six o'clock Mary Beth Toomer was probably already dead. I don't know if I can get to him tonight, before he kills somebody else. If not, I'll get him in the morning, but that'll probably be too late for somebody."

"Deb, I'm sorry, if I'd had any idea—"

"You'd have told me. I know. We can't rewrite yesterday. Thanks."

I hung up and held the receiver in my hand, shaking. *Ed Gough. He works in a rest home. He'd know how to cope with the dead weight of a woman larger than he was; he'd know how to make beds with hospital corners . . . And a Clorox fetish . . .*

Dutch, who also hadn't left yet, stared at me, and then I realized I'd been thinking out loud. Very quietly, he took a ten-dollar bill out of his billfold, laid it on my desk, and said, "Let's go."

ELEVEN

IT WASN'T THAT FAST, of course.

First we had to get warrants—an arrest warrant, to use only if we felt pretty sure we had found enough evidence to convince at least a district attorney if not a jury, and a search warrant, to use to try to get the evidence. Almost certainly Ed would sign a consent to search, but almost certainly a judge would rule, probably correctly, that Ed Gough wasn't competent to sign a consent to search.

We weren't going to be able to question him without a lawyer present. Of course, we would warn him when we got in the house, but probably the nice Miranda warning was unneeded. I couldn't imagine any court ruling him sane enough to stand trial.

But maybe the hospital would be able to keep him this time.

"What if we don't find anything?" Dutch asked me, after he returned with the signed warrants.

"I don't know," I muttered, and got out the case file. Officially, since computers, we no longer keep paper files. That is somewhat less than an actual fact. Every investigating officer I know of keeps his or her own case file, and eventually most of the material in that file finds its way to court—assuming, that is, that the case itself finds its way to court.

I had a photograph of Mary Beth Toomer, given me by her daughter. I had a photograph of Jane Stevenson, given me by her sister. I had no photograph of Corie Meeks except a Polaroid somebody from the medical examiner's office gave me, and that picture was less than suitable, in that Corie looked, well, dead.

But I tucked all three photographs into my notebook. You never know what you are going to need. You just never know.

It was nearly eight o'clock when we headed for Ed Gough's house. I had virtually no hope of finding him there. If he wasn't, I'd already decided, we'd serve the search warrant anyway, and if we found the evidence we expected to find—and probably even if we didn't—Dutch and I would sit right there in his house and wait for him to come home.

He was home. We couldn't—at least I couldn't—imagine why.

Sitting in the car outside, looking at the lights inside and the moving figure, Dutch said, "You sure?"

"Yes. Aren't you?"

"Yes, I guess. But why not tonight?"

"I don't know," I said. "I was wondering that myself."

"It was a rhetorical question."

"So glad you told me."

We got out of the car, after notifying the dispatcher where we were. If we weren't back on the air within five minutes, there'd be backups en route.

Dutch knocked on the door. Ed turned on the porch light, opened the door, and looked out at us. Or more precisely, out at me. "I fed the cats," he told me.

"That's nice," I said.

"But who'll feed them tomorrow, if you lock me up tonight?"

"I'll find somebody who'll feed them."

"They're nice cats. Is that cat still mad?"

"That which cat?"

"That cat you were carrying. Is he still mad?"

"No. He feels better now." That wasn't exactly true. Satin was sitting in his cage swearing at the universe when we left the office. But I'd figure out something to do with him.

It was interesting that Ed knew Satin was male. You certainly couldn't see through the cage, which was opaque except for the small barred area at the front. You could barely see enough to tell he (the cat, not Ed) was Siamese. Which suggested that Ed had seen the cat before, that he was able to guess what cat I was taking into the police station.

"Did you put the cat in jail?"

"No. You can't arrest cats. Anyway, he didn't do anything bad."

Dutch was tired of this. He held up the search warrant. "You know what this is?"

Ed's gaze shifted to gaze at the paper. "No. Does it mean you're going to lock me up?"

"Maybe. But right now it means we get to look all over your house."

"Oh," Ed said. "You could do that anyway."

"We wanted to be sure we were legal. Now we're coming in."

Ed backed away from the door, and belatedly I realized we needed a backup. Somebody had to keep Ed corralled while Dutch and I did the searching. I got on the radio and checked in with dispatch—it was time to do that anyway—and about two minutes later a black-and-white pulled up behind the detective car. Patrolman Ray Wilson got out. I had worked with him before; he's pretty levelheaded. That helped.

"Ray," I said, "this is Ed Gough."

Ray, his hand resting lightly, nonthreateningly, on his baton, nodded, "Hi, Ed."

"Hi, Ray," Ed said, staring fixedly at his feet.

"Ray, we—Dutch and I—are going to be searching Ed's house. I want you to sit in there in his kitchen with him while we do. The kitchen is really clean, because he was scrubbing the floor with Clorox this afternoon, so it's really the best place to sit. And Ed may tell you about his cats. Signal sixteen," I added quietly, as the cats, a couple of nondescript tabbies, curled around my legs.

Signal sixteen means demented person. Ray nodded. "They're nice-looking cats," he said. "Why don't you come in here and tell me about them?"

We started in the living room. The furniture looked about the age of the furniture in Jane's house, and as well kept. There was a large, square cabbage-rose carpet on the floor; it stopped about six inches from the edges of the hardwood floor, ending with a row of frayed fringe. There was nothing on, under, behind, or inside anything. At least nothing that didn't belong there.

We moved Ray and Ed in there long enough to check the kitchen, for all the good that didn't do, and then we let them back into the kitchen. Ed started making coffee.

I didn't want to drink it.

The bathroom had a white hamper, white towels, white fixtures, and a white floor. It didn't look sanitary. It looked vaguely sinister. But probably that was only because of my preconceptions about Ed.

Ed's bedroom—the only one in the house besides the one we'd seen earlier in the day—was equally, and equally depressingly, clean and orderly.

That meant the only place left to tackle was that ghastly other bedroom.

Dutch started at the dresser. I started at the closet.

That didn't work. We have no place to put anything.

We both made new starts, this time at the bed. We removed the pile of magazines. Removed the old bedding, some of which was so fragile it ripped. Removed the mattress to look between it and the springs. Turned the mattress over to look at the underside of it. Looked at the springs. We didn't need to turn them over because they weren't box springs, they were plain old coil springs, badly rusted. Looked under the bed. Removed old, dusty, moldy shoes, socks and slippers. Then put the bed back together and started piling on top of it everything that we finished with.

We returned to the original plan, now that we had some place to put things. Dutch checked the dresser. On the dresser. In the dresser. Under the dresser. Pulled out the drawers to see if there was anything caught behind or underneath them.

I checked the closets. The hanging clothes. The shelves. The floor.

If either one of us found anything that hadn't been the property of Ed's sister, dead nearly thirty years, we couldn't tell it.

That brought us to the array of clothes attached to the walls. All those green dresses.

We took every one down and checked it carefully. There was no green cotton paisley with purple blotches. There was no dark green woven jersey with a jewel neckline. No solid green wool dress, with or without an emerald silk scarf.

"You still sure?" Dutch asked me.

"I'm still sure." I got the pictures out of my purse and headed for the kitchen, then paused, unsure as to exactly how to proceed. Finally I repeated the Miranda warning I'd given Ed while we were waiting for Ray to arrive. "Do you understand what that means?"

"Does it mean you're gonna lock me up?"

"Probably. Depends partly on what you tell us."

"I want you to lock me up."

I put the picture of Mary Beth Toomer on the table in front of him. "Do you know her?"

"Oh, yeah, I killed her. She had on a green dress."

Behind me I could hear Dutch muttering profanity.

"Did you take her green dress?" I asked.

"Yeah," Ed said. "I thought she might want it."

"She who? You thought who might want it?"

"Her," Ed said.

Dutch muttered again. "You shouldn't say bad words," Ed told him.

"You're right," Dutch said. "I shouldn't."

"After you took her dress," I said, "what did you do then?"

"I gave her a bath," Ed said.

"You gave her a bath," Dutch repeated.

"Yeah. I gave her a bath. It isn't nice for ladies to go to bed without their bath."

"After you gave her a bath, then what?"

"I put powder on her. It smelled pretty. Then I put
〔h〕er nightgown on her. I made the bed up real nice like
〔sh〕e taught me." (The second "she," I surmised was his
〔si〕ster—the same "she" who might want the dress.)
〔T〕hen I put her in bed. And I cleaned her house up all
〔ni〕ce and clean. She didn't have a cat. The other lady
〔ha〕d a cat. That other lady didn't."

〔 〕I put the other two pictures on the table. "Which
〔on〕e had a cat?"

〔 〕Without hesitation, he indicated Corie. "She had a
〔ca〕t. I fed her cat. I left her door open so the cat could
〔co〕me in."

"Did this lady have a cat?" I pointed to Jane.

"No." He wrinkled his nose. "And she was real
〔di〕rty. I had to give her two baths."

"Did she have a green dress?"

"It wasn't a nice green dress."

"Did you scrub her floors?" I asked.

"I always scrub floors. Floors get dirty."

"But you missed a spot of blood on her bathroom
〔fl〕oor..." I stopped.

〔 〕He was shaking his head vigorously. "No blood,"
〔h〕e said. "No blood. Blood is nasty. No blood."

"But..." I began. And then I stopped to think.
〔T〕here'd been two women—Jane's boss and Jane's
〔si〕ster—in the house when the body was discovered.
〔Ei〕ther one of them could have been on her period. Ei-

ther one of them could have gone to the bathroom
could have been too agitated to notice a slight acc
dent. This certainly wouldn't be the first time, or th
last, that a police officer, in this or any other depar
ment, had gone haring after a clue that wasn't a clu
at all. I'd find out later, by discreet inquiry, whic
woman it was, just so I could tie up all the loose end
For now I had other questions to ask.

"Will you show me their dresses?" I asked.

"Whose dresses?"

"These ladies' dresses."

"Are you going to take them away?"

"Probably, yes."

"What if she wants them?" Ed asked, soundir
very agitated.

*I'd give a lot to know who this "she" he keeps tal
ing about is,* I thought. *Is it his sister? Or who el
could it be?*

"Then I'll give them back to her," I said. "But rig
now I need to take them to the police station."

"Why?"

"They'll help us be able to lock you up."

"Oh," Ed said. He thought a minute. Then
opened a kitchen drawer. We all stood, watching hi
closely, but Dutch had already checked that drawe
and all Ed got out was a flashlight.

He led us out the back door, into a gazebo in the
ackyard. "She likes to sit there," he said. "She
oesn't like to come in."

Beside me, Dutch swore. I put my hands over my
outh for a moment; it was Ray who stood quite still,
s eyes on Ed, as Dutch and I stepped forward to look
the skeleton lying on the chaise longue, the skele-
n with the broken neck and the mass of long brown
air and the faded, tattered green dress.

And at the gazebo itself, its walls festooned with
een dresses. Most of them had Goodwill price tags
them. Most. But not all.

The expensive wool dress, complete with the emer-
d silk scarf and the emerald scarf pin, didn't. Nei-
er did the green woven jersey, or the cotton paisley
th purple splotches.

O, IT WASN'T his sister, as Dutch and I both thought
start with. His sister was still where she'd been for
ore than a quarter of a century, buried in the Gough
mily plot. We never were able to find out who this
oman was. Except that she looked like his sister, ex-
pt that she was the "other one" that Ed, in his more
cid moments, had insisted over and over for the last
ven years that he had killed. The one who had rot-
d in this gazebo, lain in the gazebo summer and
nter, night and day, while we ignored his stories or
oked only into the front of his house.

But all that was a long time later, after Susan can
up to my office that night to join the court-appointe
attorney to help me question Ed Gough.

"Why?" Susan asked, after we'd established
much as we could about the skeleton.

"She said she could make me well," Ed said.

"Which one?" I laid the pictures back out on t
table in the jail.

"That one." He pointed to Jane Stevenson. "S
said she could make me well, so I'd stop wanting
kill ladies. And she didn't."

"So you killed her."

"She was wearing a green dress," he said. "I did
kill her till she was wearing a green dress."

"Was that why you didn't kill anybody betwe
Jane and Corie?" I pointed to pictures. "Between t
one and that one?"

"She wouldn't wear a green dress," he said vaguel

"You wouldn't kill her till she wore a green dress"

"Uh-huh."

"What about this one?" I pointed to Corie Meek

"She wouldn't lock me up."

"And this one?"

"She wouldn't lock me up either." He looked at n
"You wouldn't lock me up either. It was your tur
But you never would wear a green dress. They wc
green dresses."

For a minute I thought I was going to vomit. I was
at close.

Yes, I'm always armed. But only when I'm awake,
t when I'm asleep.

Then sanity reasserted itself. He wouldn't have got-
a at me, not with my husband, son, and pit bull-
g.

He looked at Susan. "You wouldn't wear a green
ess either."

With perfect aplomb, Susan replied, "I don't like
en dresses."

"Ladies are supposed to wear green dresses."

"Was that the real reason you killed them?" Susan
ked.

There was a long silence. Then, finally, Ed an-
ered, "I had to make them lock me up."

"You killed the ladies in the green dresses so some-
dy would lock you up?"

"Yeah. I didn't know what else to do. I was afraid
as going to start killing everybody."

"Sometimes the system breaks down," Susan said.

"What does that mean?"

"It means we should have locked you up. All right,
know what you do when ladies don't lock you up.
at do you do when men won't lock you up?"

"Only ladies," he said. "Ladies are supposed to
k me up."

"What was your mother like?"

"She locked me up."

"When did she lock you up?"

"When I was bad."

"Where did she lock you up?"

"In the pantry. In the dark." His face twisted as he was about to cry. "She had on a green dress."

"Your mother?"

"No, her."

"Your sister?"

"Yes. She had on a green dress. I wasn't trying to bad. I just wanted to look. That's all. I just wanted look."

"How old were you then?"

"I was six."

"How old was your sister?"

"She was eleven. Her dress got blood on it. I want to know how it got blood on it. It was a pretty dr but it got blood on it."

"Where did it get blood on it?"

"Where she sat down. She made her burn the dr and she cried."

"Your mother made your sister burn the dress a your sister cried?"

"I was in the pantry. I just wanted to look."

"Thank you," Susan said. "We're going to le you alone and let you get some rest now."

"Will somebody feed my cats?"

"I'll feed your cats," I said.

Back in our office, Susan said, "He's never going to be coherent. But I've got enough of the picture."

"I think I do, too."

Satin yowled in the corner, and Susan ambled over to look at him. "This his cat?" There was real surprise in her voice.

"No, it's Corie Meeks's cat."

"Now that I can believe." She opened the carrier, and I held my breath, waiting for the cat to start growling. The cat crawled out of the cage and climbed up into Susan's lap, purring loudly. "Hi, cat," she said, and looked at me. "What's his name?"

"Corie Meeks called him Satan," I said, "but I think Satin's a better name."

Susan chuckled. "You get more Mormon every day. You want to come home with me, Satin?"

Satin purred.

Now all I had to do was find homes for two tabbies who were used to the smell of Clorox.

Well, I managed. Olead and Becky took them both. They're pretty patient cats. They'd have to be, with a toddler and another baby on the way, but Becky says actually they help—they give Jeffrey something to do besides draw on the wall.

I did ask Olead how in the world somebody like Ed Gough had gotten into Mensa. "He took a test," Olead replied.

"When?" I asked suspiciously.

He shrugged. "How should I know? It might have been thirty years ago. But I don't really think he's ever been much saner than he is right now. I've been trying to tell you, Deb. Intelligence and sanity are two completely different things."

"But he hasn't even been to college, has he?"

"Intelligence and education," Olead said patiently, "are two entirely different things. We've got six-year-olds in Mensa."

Well. That put a different light on things. I'd been thinking. A test that made Isaac Asimov nervous, a test that Samuel Barrett couldn't pass—but a test *Ed Gough* could pass? Really. I didn't need to be scared of that.

So I took it.

And you know what?

I passed.

But I'm darned if I'm going to let Olead talk me into going to the meetings.

Finders KEEPERS

ELIZABETH TRAVIS

AN INSPECTOR NICK TREVELLYAN MYSTERY

HOPE AGAINST HOPE

SUSAN B. KELLY

First Time In Paperback

DEATH IN THE FAMILY

Aidan Hope is bludgeoned to death in his hotel room in the hamlet of Little Hopford. The prime suspect is Alison Hope, the victim's cousin, a brash, beautiful, wealthy businesswoman who inherits sole ownership of a lucrativ software business. Alison maintains she bought Aidan out years ago. So wh had Aidan suddenly appeared to claim his rights and his money?

Fighting his growing desire for the red-haired Alison, Detective Inspector Nick Trevellyan undertakes the investigation. Alison has no alibi . . . and every reason to have killed her cousin. But as Aidan's unscrupulous past comes to light, and a second body turns up, Trevellyan begins to hope that Alison is innocent . . . although that may mean she'll be the next to die.

"A pleasant diversion and a promise of good things to come."

—*Library Journa*

W☮RLDWIDE LIBRARY®

A Sheila Travis Mystery

MURDER

in the Charleston Manner

PATRICIA
HOUCK
SPRINKLE

First Time in Paperback

A LETHAL DOSE OF SOUTHERN COMFORT

"Trouble follows that woman like fleas follow a dog," her father had always said about Aunt Mary. Sheila Travis ruefully agrees when she is dispatched by her colorful aunt to Charleston to "investigate" some mysterious accidents occurring at the historic home of Mary's childhood friends, Dolly and Marion.

Sheila's hostesses are a monument to Southern hospitality, and though a master at protocol, the former ambassador's wife feels boorish by comparison. But this isn't a social visit—Sheila has a job to do even if she's initially inclined to write the accidents off as coincidence. The first murder changes her mind....

"A plethora of likely suspects, all with motives, means and opportunity."

—*Booklist*

A PORT SILVA MYSTERY

GRANDMOTHER'S
HOUSE

JANET LAPIERRE

First Time In Paperback

PORT SILVA—LAND TO KILL FOR?

Situated on California's beautiful northern coast, Port Silva ha
escaped the rash of land developers eating up the state's prim
real estate. But when a posh San Diego firm finally offers sma
fortunes to persuade the people on historic Finn Lane to sell ou
everyone jumps at the chance. Except thirteen-year-old Pete
Birdsong. The house belonged to his grandmother. He's not se
ing. Charlotte, his mother, stands adamantly beside him.

But how far will Petey go to defend his home?

"LaPierre is something else ... real talent."
— *Mystery Readers of America Journ*

Hard Luck

A Cat Marsala Mystery

Barbara D'Amato

First
Time in
Paperback

HIGH STAKES

Chicago journalist Cat Marsala has just begun her assignment on the state lottery when murder falls into the picture—literally—as a lottery official takes a leap in the middle of the multistate lottery conference.

Suicide... or murder? It's curious to Cat—and to the police—that the guy took his mighty plunge right before his meeting with her. Especially curious since he'd hinted at some great exposé material, like "misappropriation" of lottery funds.

"Cat Marsala is one of the most appealing new sleuths to come along in years."
—*Nancy Pickard*

ZERO *at the* BONE

A KATHERINE DRISCOLL MYSTERY

First Time in Paperback

Mary Willis Walker

UNSUSPECTING PREY

It had been thirty-one years since Katherine Driscoll had seen her fathe
Then he sent a cryptic letter. He knew she was in trouble—about to lo
her home, her dog kennel and her beloved championship show dog, R
to creditors. He was offering his help.

Katherine went to meet him at the Austin Zoo where he was senior keep
of the large cats. But she just missed him—he'd been mauled to death I
a tiger.

With nothing to go on but a key and receipt from a storage warehous
Katherine took a job at the zoo and started probing into her father's I
zarre death.

> "Walker is terrific at goosebumps."
> —*The Philadelphia Inquir*